Copyright © 1995 by Spiro Athanas

All rights reserved

First Printing, 1995

St. Spyridon Press, a division of Prince Management Services, Inc.
Bloomington, Indiana

A Bag of Oranges was published in the Ball State University *Forum* magazine (1973), and subsequently in an anthology entitled *Ethnic American Short Stories* (1975), edited by Katherine D. Newman. However, the author maintains all rights to this story and to all other stories in this book.

The cover art and all other illustrations were created by the author on an IBM computer. Copyright © 1995 by Spiro Athanas. All rights reserved.

This is a work of fiction. Names, characters, places and incidents are either the product of the author's imagination or are used fictionally. Any resemblence to actual places, events or persons living or dead is entirely coincidental.

The Voice of the Titans
and other stories

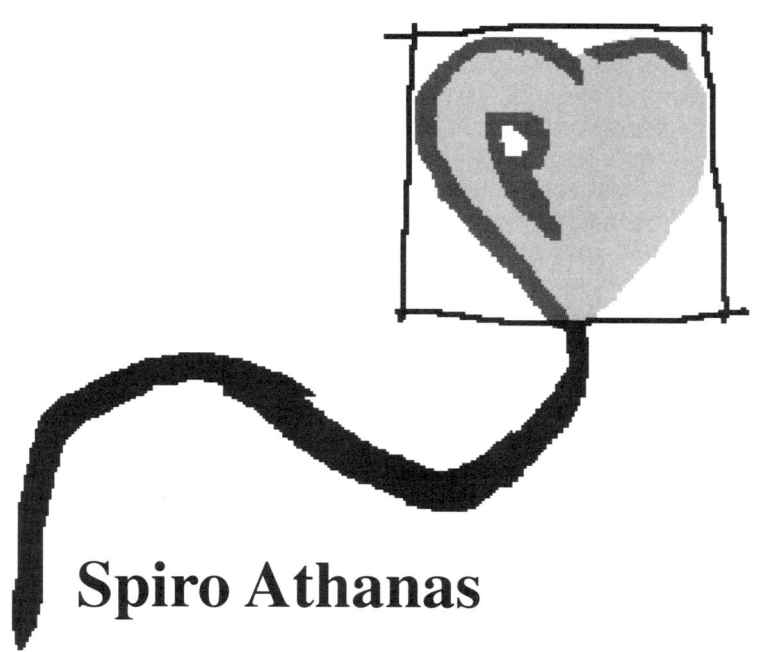

Spiro Athanas

CONTENTS

A Bag Of Oranges..................................1

Five Seconds Of Sweet Perfection.....................9

No Laughing On The Sixth Floor......................15

I Came Here To Shoot Somebody......................17

Why Do Birds Sing?..............................30

Killer Kardonoway...............................46

What Mary Wanted.............................49

The Lesson....................................60

Weights And Measures..........................68

The Voice Of The Titans.........................72

In The Desert

In the desert
I saw a creature, naked, beastial,
Who squatting upon the ground,
Held his heart in his hands,
And ate of it.
I said, "Is it good, friend?"
"It is bitter— bitter," he answered,
"But I like it
Because it is bitter,
And because it is my heart."

Stephen Crane

A BAG OF ORANGES

The city market was crowded. The boy Nikos Pappanoulos bobbed and weaved among the shoppers. He held a blue cloth sack tightly; his father walking briskly ahead carried three others. Skip stepping, the ten-year-old tried to keep up with his father's long stride. Stavro Pappanoulos strode easily, cutting a smooth path through the thick crowd like a plow turning earth. Something about the set of his shoulders said, "Step aside," and people did. The boy was proud of his father's stocky strength, yet at the same time it made him uneasy.

Nikos loved the market, loved coming to shop with his father on Saturday mornings. He loved the smells and bright Fall colors of apples, pears, pumpkins, of the fresh fruits and vegetables in the October morning air. The market was like a magic farm indomitably growing and prospering in the heart of the rotting slum.

The boy's father knew many of the truck farmers who displayed their colorful harvests in pyramids, bunches or boxes in the open-air market. He was especially friendly with a gray, old Albanian who hawked strawberries.

"*Lulustrouthia! Lulustrouthia!*" the gaunt, hook-nosed farmer yelled. And it worked. No one could hear that cry against the other banal sounds without investigating.

"*Lulustrouthia?* That's Albanian for the freshest, juiciest, sweetest stawberries ever grown," was his stock reply, uttered rather condescendingly to the fat matron who stood before him. "Fifteen cents a box." She bought a box and waddled away, biting off the stems of the unwashed strawberries and popping the fruit into her mouth.

"Twenty cents for two?" The boy's father plunked down two shiny, new 1955 dimes next to the rows of boxes overflowing with plump strawberries.

"No, no, Stavro Pappanoulos, thirty cents for two. Two times fifteen is thirty." He said this distinctly and rocked back on his heels apparently delighted with his arithmetic.

"Twenty - two."

"Thirty."

"Twenty-five."

"Sold!" The old Albanian adroitly slid the dimes into his money pouch.

"Sonofabitch," his father mumbled as he flipped a nickel to the Albanian.

"Move away from the stand now Stavro Pappanoulos, I don't want people to see how you rob me— *Lulustrouthia!* HEY LULUSTRRROUTHIA!"

The boy watched and listened to this dialogue, intrigued— and a little frightened. But the smile on his father's lips as they walked away reassured him.

When the sacks were at last filled and the boy held the one bag of oranges that could not be coaxed into any of them, he and his father made their weekly visit to the Greek coffee house across the street. To get there they had to pass through the enclosed end of the U-shaped market, the only part the boy didn't like. It was poorly lighted. The chicken house, butcher shop and fish market all reeked of death. The boy ran ahead of his father, out the double door and again into the light. He waited at the curb for his father. Stavro took his hand and strode into the street, defying traffic. He seemed to delight in making cars stop to let him pass.

In the coffee house the boy sat on a corner of his father's chair. Stavro unbuttoned his pin-striped suit coat and removed his gray hat. As he sipped dark, viscous coffee, the boy ate from the bag of peanuts given him by his uncle Peter Pappas, proprietor of the coffee house. Peter was Stavro's brother, but had shortened his name for "business purposes."

The boy, dark and quiet and shy, watched the men at the other tables playing backgammon and pinochle. The men at Stavro's table spoke in low confiding tones.

"Michales is dying, you know." Peter clenched the stub of his cigar between his teeth.

"It's that woman," a slight bald man chirped. The boy didn't know him. "He's not enough man for Aphrodite."

"No one is enough man for Aphrodite, eh Stavro?" Peter nudged his brother.

"Old ladies, all of you. Gossiping old ladies." Stavro spat between the space in his front teeth into a cuspidor, smiling mischieviously. The talk continued. They spoke of politics and business and gambling. Stavro sat like a rock with his legs corralling the four brimming cloth sacks. He lit a Fatima and put one of his hands gently on the boy's head. The boy enjoyed the talk and sometimes felt he was being allowed to hear all the secrets of the world, and was only mildly frustrated by the mysteries he could not understand.

"Time to go, Nikos," Stavro ran his fingers through his own thick, black hair and put on his hat. "I need a haircut," he said, to no one in particular.

Nikos was glad to be in the fresh air again when they left. It was even sweeter after being in the mustiness of his uncle's tiny coffee house. And he ran ahead of his father again, this time to the bus stop at the corner.

The bus was crowded. There were many elderly women and young girls with bright packages, returning from downtown shopping trips; but only a few men. It was mid-afternoon in October, and the bus was uncomfortably warm. The boy sat beside his father on the long seat at the rear.

The bus jolted over the city streets, jerking to an abrupt halt at nearly every corner, picking up and surrendering passengers. The boy was holding the oranges so lightly that when the bus lurched into motion after one of the stops, the bag was thrust forward and five oranges bounded into the aisle. Like pinballs, they careened off the brackets and poles. The boy regained control of the bag before any more could escape, and his father scampered down the aisle chasing oranges.

On his hands and knees, Stavro Pappanoulos ducked beneath a seat on which two old ladies sat, to their mild humor and fussy dismay, and emerged with three of the oranges. The two others had rolled farther down the aisle. He picked up one, and as he started for the other, a neatly dressed young man reached down from where he was sitting and took it up. Stavro quickly grabbed the young man's wrist and began squeezing. The man gasped slightly, opening his mouth in a grimace of pain and apparent disbelief. Stavro tightened his grip and stared menacingly into the pink face. Finally the young man's grasp was loosened by the pressure and he dropped the orange. Stavro picked it up and walked back to his seat at the rear of the bus. The young man stared after him, his mouth still open, rubbing his wrist briskly.

"You know," he began, "I mean anyone could see— I wasn't about to steal your precious orange."

A wave of laughter ran through the bus. Stavro Pappanoulos looked at the man mildly and popped the five oranges back into the boy's bag, carefully folding over the top. He settled himself in his seat once again and looked satisfied. The young man shrugged his shoulders and turned around. There were a few whispers and a few more smiles.

The boy felt every whisper piercing his skin, every smile was a slap. His ears burned with embarrassment and shame. The remainder of the trip was an agony. Even the backs of the old grey heads, the light pony tails, the clean shaven necks seemed to mock the boy. For the first time in his life he hated his father.

At their stop, the boy and his father had to pass the young man to get to the door. The boy, mortified, walked by stiffly, staring straight ahead, his head ringing, tears in his eyes. He felt the shadow and weight of his father behind him, placid and unashamed. Oh how he hated him and his smug, foreign stupidity. Why did he have to be *his* father?

Once on the sidewalk the boy dared not look back at the bus as it coughed and whined away for fear it too would mock him. He walked behind his father now, crying silent hot tears. His father turned once and must have noticed the tears, but said nothing.

At the gate to their front yard the boy's older sister bounded out to greet them and leaped with remarkable agility onto her father's back. Viki, who was twelve, snuggled her head in Stavro's neck and kissed him affectionately. And as they both laughed, Stavro carried her up the stairs to the porch where the boy caught up with them. Viki jumped from her father's back, snatched the bag of oranges from her brother and disappeared into the house. Stavro put his bags down for a moment and placed a hand on the boy's head.

The boy sprang to him, putting his arms around his father's neck and wrapping his legs around his hard body. In this way, they arrived at the kitchen— the boy still clinging to his amused father.

"Look at my monkey," Stavro said to his wife. And the boy was delighted to be his father's monkey again. It was so easy and natural he could scarcely believe the emotions he experienced moments ago were real. Had he *really* thought he hated his father?

The boy's mother was looking at the oranges Viki had given her. She took a few out of the bag.

"And what happened to these, Stavro? Did you sit on them on the way home?"

"Some dropped. It is of no importance." Stavro looked at the boy.

"Well, we can't eat these, but I can use them for juice. Viki, why don't you go to the store and buy a dozen for Poppa's lunches?" Viki frowned, but she knew it was not a question. She went to her mother's purse in the hall closet, removed a dollar, and left for the store.

"And you Nikos, be a good boy and bring in the cans from the alley. If you leave them they will get dented worse than they are."

II

The late afternoon sun, subdued by the October mist, hung quietly just above the horizon. It was getting dark earlier. The boy sent a flattened bottle cap skimming down the vacant alley. Then he carried in the empty battered trash cans, one at a time. He stopped after his third and last trip to watch a lone gray pigeon gracefully circle his back yard. In a flutter of furious motion the fat bird ascended to the gutter atop the three-story house and settled gently on the edge. It flicked its nervous head from side to side. And the boy remembered the trap his father had made on the roof: kernels of corn leading to a chicken wire box. He remembered pigeon soup. There had been the need; hard times.

He felt a sudden chill, an inner void; and he began to run. Up the brick walk and over the mound, the swelling where the roots of the gnarled oak had had their say; up the porch stairs, two, three steps at a time; the agile, plastic ten year-old, a piece of tempered wire.

Near the top of a second flight of stairs, still trying to outrun his own insides, the boy heard the soft, familiar
voices: his mother and father as they communed over coffee. He stopped running. Slowly, carefully he walked the brown crack in the flowered linoleum down the hall to the kitchen. A sheer drop of ten

thousand feet on either side.

"Did you bring in the cans?" The boy nodded and his mother smiled her approval. She wiped a loose, dark hair from her smooth brow.

The boy moved from the doorway to the table. His father sat there easily, his legs spread. And the boy remembered the coffee house; remembered the mischief in his father's smile as the men spoke of "Aunt" Aphrodite; remembered the dying Michales.

"Coffee?"

"Yes, black coffee," the boy said, quietly.

"So it's *black* coffee is it; a man's drink." His mother, already moving toward the cupboard— petite, slender in a bright print dress. Dark smiling eyes, affectionate, maternal. She filled a hand-painted demitasse from a copper pot at the stove and brought it to the boy.

He sipped. It was bitter, the price of being a man.

"I'm going now to get a haircut. Borsch will be closed in half an hour." The boy's father finished his coffee in one long swallow and pushed himself up heavily. Thick, dark, quiet— he spoke a familiar word to his wife, a parting— and he was gone. The boy sat in the chair, in the warmth of his father's body, and watched his mother clear the table.

"Why don't you play outside, now?"

"Nobody's around."

"Viki will be back soon."

He watched his mother wash the cups at the sink. And he thought of his "Aunt" Aphrodite, again. Aphrodite Skouras was not a relation, but she was a very close friend of the family. She read fortunes in the swirling patterns the coffee grounds made in empty cups. On more than one occasion the boy had sat in a corner of the kitchen and watched the cluster of women and girls, clinging to her every word. He had watched amused, amazed and, sometimes, frightened. Before long they would discover him, usually it was his mother, for she was the most skeptical and paid the least attention, and he was ushered from the room. For days afterwards he would hear talk of "Aunt" Aphrodite's predictions. Now he remembered that her last visit had caused a pall to settle over the company. Even the bright sarcasm and laughter of his mother seemed false in the face of the dark future Aphrodite must have forecast.

The boy's mother began to hum a particularly gay Greek tune as she worked at the sink. But somewhere, deep in the boy's mind the song was transformed into a wail. And then it broke upon a distant reality. Suddenly the room was filled with the sound— screaming terrifically, ominously. And then, abruptly, it subsided to a low, soft moan.

"Go to the window and see." His mother, urgent, always frightened by sirens. She listened intently.

The boy rushed to a living room window, pushed aside the long hand-crocheted curtain and parted the blind. He saw nothing unusual in the street below except the autos backed up, bumper to bumper. But it was Saturday and theirs was a busy street.

Back in the kitchen he said nothing. The wailing sound was gone. His mother wiped the worn oilcloth that covered the solid oak table. She stopped midway in the arc of a smooth stroke, "Shhh."

The boy had not uttered a sound. He held his breath. His mother lifted her head and seemed to prick her ears listening to something he could not hear. She held the hand with which she sought to quiet him poised above the table —motionless. "What?" The boy said, "I don't hear anything."

"Nothing. Nothing at all." His mother finished wiping the table and went back to her work. The boy saw her knitted brow reflected in the mirror above the sink. She did not hum any more.

The boy sat in his father's chair sipping the thick coffee; both had lost their warmth. He watched his mother's efficient hands preparing *moussaka* at the sink for their evening meal and thought of nothing.

The noise of the front door slamming against the wall echoed violently in the hollow stairwell. The boy had often heard it slammed shut, but this was a different, urgent sound which compelled both him and his mother to rush to the stairs. "Momma, oh Momma, Momma," it was a thin hysterical voice that came to them. They watched Viki, alert and afraid. Her mouth formed the words but she did not, could not speak. Her body writhed and her face twisted but no sound came. Finally, "It's Poppa. Oh, Momma, Poppa."

His mother's eyes were glazed black, wild with terror. She clasped her hands together and ran down the stairs. The boy, rooted to the spot, faced his sister. He began to shake. His neck felt stiff. Then he saw the empty bag Viki clutched to her breast as she rocked side to side. The bottom had torn out. She followed his eyes to the tear. "The oranges. I lost them. Oh Poppa." The tears now began to flow down her flushed face, from terrified eyes.

The boy wanted to know, but he did not dare ask. He watched and waited. Viki put the bag on the dining room table and turned back to face the boy. He still could not move. "I saw his hat. The people were in a circle and there was Poppa's hat. I didn't believe it was Poppa's at first. But I knew it was. I knew it was his grey hat." She paused and sobbed and wiped the tears from her frightened face. "Then I saw Poppa. He wasn't bleeding. He looked okay. Like he was asleep. Like he was lying in the street asleep. "Nikos, Nikos." She went to the motionless, terrified boy and put her hands on his shoulders. "Poppa's been hit by a car, Nikos. He couldn't talk or see, but maybe it's not bad. There wasn't any blood. He looked okay, Nikos. He's okay." She began to choke on her fear, her deep hurt.

The boy felt a drop of perspiration slip down his side. He could hear and feel his heart work faster, faster. And he broke away from his sister, running, stumbling down the stairs to the front porch.

He could make nothing out of what he saw in the street. There was a car double-parked in the next block, but police and people milled about on the corner. He could not see his mother among them. Too late, he was confused and bewildered. He had made up his mind to run down to the corner. But he found he couldn't run. And then he knew he didn't want to run. He didn't want to reach the corner —ever. Half way down the block he saw them, the oranges his sister had dropped. Most of them were in a little pile by the curb. But one was in the center of the sidewalk, near the corner.

Of a sudden, a man who had been part of the small crowd which seemed unable to leave the scene of the excitement, though there was nothing left to see... of a sudden a young man broke from the crowd and picked up the orange near the corner. He tested it in the palm of his hand, and as if finding it acceptable, turned to walk up the street, away from the boy.

A neighbor, an old woman, noticed the boy and made a comforting gesture, a movement toward him. Seeing this, Nikos began to run; past the woman and the corner. In the middle of the next block he caught up with the young man who had picked up the orange. Without breaking stride, the boy leaped onto the man's back, his small fists flailing wildly.

"That's my orange!" he screamed. "Give me my orange!"

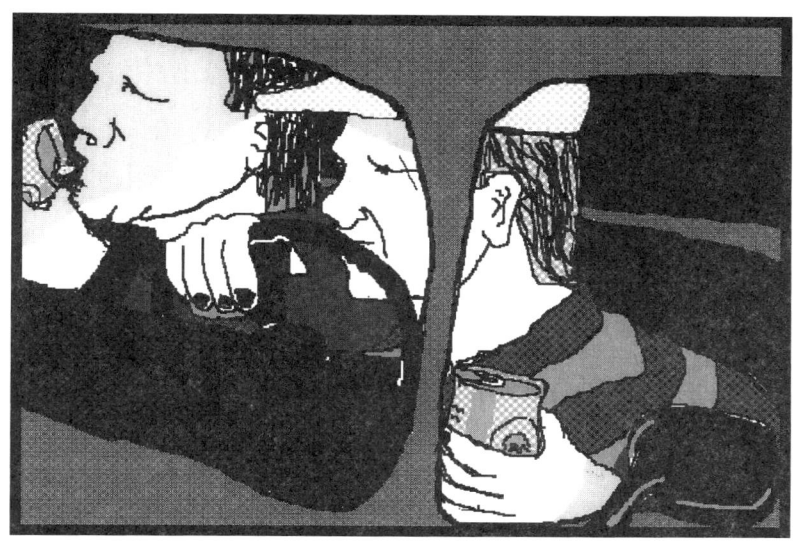

FIVE SECONDS OF SWEET PERFECTION

I picked up Guy Sowders at about eight-thirty. It was a warm June night, but a light breeze was blowing off the river. We stopped at the Hog and Frog Inn and bought a six-pack of Bud. I figured we'd finish it off by the time I drove to Busch Stadium and found a place to park. We weren't in any hurry. We planned to watch the middleweights and the light-heavies on the undercard. But what we were really going there to see was Precious Octavius Barnes fight Carl "Big Cat" Wilson for the undisputed Heavyweight Championship of the World. It was the first heavyweight championship fight ever scheduled in St. Louis, which is surprising since Sonny Liston and both the Spinks brothers lived here. But I guess St. Louis isn't really a fight town. Not like Vegas or Atlantic City or New York City.

The only reason the fight was on in St. Louis was because Precious Barnes said he wouldn't fight Wilson anywhere else. And somehow Precious and his people talked Don King into promoting the fight in their hometown. King sold the TV rights to HBO. The take was about twenty million, not counting the gate.

The story on Precious Octavius Barnes was that he'd never been knocked off his feet. *Ring* magazine said he'd had ninety-two amateur fights and ninety-two wins— seventy-eight by KO. And he was undefeated as a pro too, twenty-five wins— twenty-three KO's; W.B.C. and W.B.A. Heavyweight Champion of the World. But I knew better. And so did Guy Sowders and Sid Weintraub (the referee), and Lew Mavasi (the Champ's manager), and Precious Octavius Barnes himself, and maybe sixty or seventy assorted fight officials, handlers and spectators. We knew that on January seventeenth in 1979 when Precious and I were both sixteen years old, Precious Octavius Barnes was put down and out in his sixth amateur fight.

It was the semifinals of the St. Louis Golden Gloves novice division championship at the Homer G. Phillips Veterans Memorial Hall in North St. Louis. Guy was fighting middleweight in the same semi, and a kid named Benny Pastorini took him apart for three rounds to win the decision. That was Guy's last fight. He quit high school and went to work for Hagger Hinge that summer. And he's been there ever since. He never stopped going to the gym, though. Even after he was married and had two kids. He'd have a few beers after work and then he'd go to the gym two or three times a week, just to watch and remember.

"I hate watchin' those lightweight palookas who can't bust a balloon with their best shot," Sowders said as he unwrapped a stick of Wrigley's spearmint and folded it into his mouth. He threw the wrapper out the car window. "Now those middleweights, that's a whole another story. Georgie Cordova, who weighed one fifty-eight, same as me, dropped a dago who goes maybe two-thirty— two-forty at the Olive Street gym one day. Was you there?

"Yeah, I was there, Guy," I said. We both knew we were about to retell the same story we had told each other and a lot of other people a hundred times. "Georgie's working the light bag, wearing those bright pink trunks that were his trademark," I said.

"And this big slob walks by and says to his buddy, 'Lookit the little spic queer,'" Sowders said.

"And then Georgie, still shadow boxing, dances over to the fat ass and says, `D'jou say someteeng too me, Mon?'" I said.

"And the blimp goombah squares off, but before he can say or do anything...," Sowders began.

"Ba-bing, Ba-bang, Ba-boom...Georgie hits him with two shots to the gut and then puts him down with a perfect right uppercut," I finished the story.

"Those were the days," Sowders said. "Those were the days, Chooch," he said again, shaking his head, remembering.

Choo Choo Karpinsky was my fighting name. And Sowders, he calls me Chooch for short. He's the only one that called me that. I never understood why nobody else picked up on a nickname my best buddy calls me. I like bein' called Chooch, but everybody calls me Choo Choo. I came by the nickname because I'm only five feet-eight, but I weighed one seventy-four in my prime. So I fought the light-heavyweights, some of them a head taller than me. The only way I had a chance was to get inside and count on my strength, and my punching speed, and my stamina.

One day at the Olive Street gym, after I had turned pro, I was sparring a few rounds with this no-name newcomer and I backed him into a corner. I hammered at him with my shoulders and elbows and I was pumping my arms like a wild man. So Lew Mavasi, my manager at the time, said, "Goddamn if Stanley don't look like an old-time steam engine. Choo Choo Karpinsky." And that's the name that he hung on me; and that's the name that stuck. But, like I said, I like Chooch better.

Lew Mavasi was in *our* corner that cold January night. We were fighting out of the Twelfth Street South St. Louis Boy's Club. Even though Lew already managed a few pro fighters back then, he kind of adopted the Twelfth Street Boy's Club as a pet project. There were some good prospects at that club, and I'm not ashamed to say that I was one of the best. A real comer. Precious Barnes and I were both light heavyweights in 1979. At one seventy-one, he was giving up three pounds to me. But he was already six foot-three and there wasn't an ounce of fat on him. For two rounds and two minutes and fifty-five seconds of the third and final round, Precious Octavius Barnes hit me whenever he wanted. We were both undefeated and I'd had two more official amateur fights than he did, but I couldn't lay a glove on him.

I tried everything I knew and a bunch of tactics I made up during the fight (I tackled him at the end of the second round and was almost disqualified by Sid Weintraub, the referee). Nothing worked. I couldn't get inside; I couldn't touch him *period* if he didn't want me to. Precious kept hitting me around my right eye with his left jab, and then he would *move* to my right. And when I stepped in, he'd dig me with a hard right under the ribs. It seemed like those were the only two places he hit me all night. By the end of the second round my right eye was almost swollen shut and a deep purplish-blue bruise was spreading across my midsection.

There was a doctor at ringside and he looked me over between the second and third rounds. He shook his head and said it was Lew's call whether I answered the bell for the final round. I told Lew if he stopped the fight I'd quit boxing, and at the time I think I meant it. I've been guilty of a lot of things in my life, but nobody ever called me a quitter.

"I just wish the sumbitch would hit me someplace else besides my right eye or under the ribs," I said. And that got a rise out of Lew, who smiled his crooked smile, and decided to let me try to finish the fight.

The last round was more of the same. My right eye was just a slit and I couldn't see anything but the blur of lights and left jabs. I tried to cut off the ring, always coming forward, which was my style, but Precious was too fast and had too much reach on me. In fact, he had all the skills. He could make me miss just by pulling back his head, the way Muhammad Ali used to do in his prime.

To this day I can't tell you which was worse: the physical beating I took (I pissed blood for three days after the fight and the left side of my face didn't match the right side ever again) or the empty feeling I got that I wasn't much of a fighter— or much of a man.

That is until the last five seconds of the third round. Precious knew he had whipped me, but he also knew he couldn't put me down. He had hit me with everything he had, but I was still right there in front of him. The last thirty seconds or so he began to clown a little, I think to hide his own frustration. He stuck out his chin, faked a bolo punch, and did an imitation Ali shuffle. And then, in the last ten or fifteen seconds, he put his arms down to his sides and just danced away as I bulled forward.

But, all of a sudden, he tripped dancing back and stumbled sideways into a neutral corner. I caught him with a left hook from a perfectly planted position, which means he absorbed the full weight and force of my legs, body, arm and fist flush on his right jaw. His fighter's instinct told him I was coming with my right, and even though he was dazed, he raised his left hand to protect his jaw. But, somewhere, the place where fighting instinct lives I guess, I had already figured his defense and, instead of throwing the right, I hit him with another almost perfect left hook.

What happened next seemed as though it was happening to somebody else. I swear I saw (with my one good eye) his whole face go blank. He seemed out on his feet. And, as he dropped both arms, I pivoted and sent a crunching right cross to the left side of his jaw. I never again threw a harder or more perfectly timed combination. It was five seconds of sweet perfection. The right cross landed just as the bell sounded, and Precious Octavius Barnes dropped in slow motion like a house of cards falling in on itself.

Sid Weintraub started to count him out. When he got to three, he must have noticed that Precious was out cold because Weintraub waved his arms and called for the doctor. Precious was out for at least three minutes. In fact, I began to get worried and I went over to see how he was doing, but his corner men pushed me away. I noticed that the doctor, who was bent over Precious with a stethoscope pressed to his chest, looked worried too. When they finally lifted Barnes to his feet, his legs were so wobbly they had to prop him up on the stool in his corner.

At that time, you couldn't be saved by the bell in the Golden Gloves. But the judges decided that the knockout punch had landed after the bell had sounded. And their word was final. So Precious won his sixth amateur fight real easy on points, and I went down to my first defeat. The first of forty-two losses in my six year boxing career, four years as a pro, which was over what seems like a hundred years ago. Now I deliver Taystee Bread to food stores.

The truth is not much has gone right for me since that January night in 1979. I was married to a girl named Kelly a couple of years ago, but that didn't work out. She had long red hair so soft it almost breaks my heart to think about it. Kelly was a secretary at Conner's Ford, and she left me for some hot-shot car salesman. I guess I'm a lot like Guy in some ways. I like my Budweiser. And I still go to the Olive Street gym to watch and remember.

As the fighters were being introduced at Busch Stadium for the main event, fifteen rounds for the undisputed Heavyweight Championship of the World, we could barely see them. Guy and I were sitting in what would have been the upper tier of the left field bleachers if we were watching a baseball game: the cheap seats. Lew Mavasi was in Precious Barnes' corner and Sid Weintraub was the referee. I was watching the three of them through my binoculars as the announcer was saying, "And in this corner, wearing gold satin trunks with the black stripes, weighing two hundred and eighteen pounds, undefeated and never knocked off his feet in both his amateur and professional boxing career.. the W.B.C. and W.B.A. undisputed Heavyweight Champion of the World, Precious Octavius Barnes." When the announcer said that part about never being knocked off his feet I could swear Precious and Lew and Sid all looked up in my direction.

    I glanced over at Guy and he was grinning from ear to ear. And for a minute I had the same feeling I had on January seventeenth in 1979... only this time it was even better because I knew I wouldn't be pissing blood for three days. But after the bell rang and Precious started dancing around the slow-moving Big Cat, flicking that lightning quick jab into Wilson's face, I started feeling sad. Guy stopped the Bud man and handed me a cup of beer foaming to the brim. I drank the whole thing in three or four giant swallows without putting down the cup.

NO LAUGHING ON THE SIXTH FLOOR

Standing ten feet from the exact spot from which Lee Harvey Oswald *allegedly* fired those fateful shots on November 22, 1963, I watch my father. He looks a lot like Robert Frost did on the day of John Kennedy's inauguration, a shock of white hair straying across his craggy forehead. I remember reading that Frost had a mean streak.

"The Sixth Floor." That's what the Dallas ad agency or public relations firm charged with the task decided to name the exhibit on the sixth floor of what was the Texas School Book Depository in 1963. The City Fathers waited twenty-five years for the whole damn mess to go away. But since it would not, could not, they decided to make the sixth floor of the building into a kind of circus for tourists. And since everyone loves a circus, The Sixth Floor is crowded even though it is a rainy Wednesday afternoon in May.

"Do you think that little, skinny fart did it by himself?" My father asks, his head nodding in a palsy worse than the last time I saw him, just three months ago. We're watching one of the half-dozen or so audio-visual presentations scattered around the partitioned warehouse floor.

"I don't think it really matters," I say, knowing it will raise his hackles.

"Doesn't matter? Goddamn, Tom, I send you to SMU for half your adult life. You're supposed to be the head of molecule research..."

"Molecular," I say, correcting him without thinking.

"...or whatever the hell it is and you mean to tell me you're not even curious?" My father wipes the spittle collecting at the right corner of his mouth with the back of his knobby steelworker's hand. His face is turning crimson.

"Take it easy, dad. I didn't say I wasn't curious. What I said was, I don't think it matters. Those are two different concepts, different states of mind," I say, half-smiling, egging him on.

"Concepts. States of mind. My raggedy ass. We're talking about the assassination of the President of the United States. You think that commie piss ant could've hit a moving target (twice, mind you) with a piece-of-shit eye-talian rifle from that window over there? Yes or no?" My father demands, pointing toward the glass enclosed space that enshrines *the* window, baring his lower teeth as he frowns. Those teeth are false and, therefore, terrifically white and perfectly even. They look ridiculous, almost comic .

I watch him glare at me for a moment, his tirade having attracted the attention of several bystanders. Then I look down as though I'm pondering his question. Finally I say, "What I'd really like to know is why we call the two most infamous American presidential assassins by their full given names. I mean, why is it always John *Wilkes* Booth and Lee *Harvey* Oswald, never just John Booth or just Lee Oswald?"

My father stares at me in exaggerated astonishment for several seconds. And then he claps me on the shoulder and begins to laugh. He's laughing loudly and now everyone seems to be looking our way. I notice that Zapruder's eight millimeter home movie of Kennedy's motorcade moving through Dealy Plaza is being played in slow motion on the screen of the TV near us. But I can't help it; I begin laughing too, and as my father leans into me, I put my right arm around his shrinking body in an half-embrace.

Some men come to know their fathers late, I think, as a uniformed exhibit guard (a Texas Ranger?) walks toward us with a disapproving expression on his officious face. They cut away before the video reaches the part where the top of Kenndy's head is blown off, anyway.

I CAME HERE TO SHOOT SOMEBODY

Bobby Dwyer's wife left him on a Friday. He came home from work and found the pink note neatly scotch-taped to the formica kitchen table. The dishes from two days' meals had been shoved back to form a semi-circle of cleared table. After he read the note twice, Bobby found himself concentrating on the handwriting instead of what his wife had written. Ellen's handwriting was labored and elaborate like that of a girl of thirteen. She dotted her "i"s with big circles and ended almost every word with a curlicue. Bobby liked her handwriting. It made him think of the way Ellen looked and smelled after a hot bath: young and pink and feminine... and his.

Bobby began to cry. And then, of a sudden, he bolted out the apartment door, running, stumbling down the stairs to his car. Without looking, he backed wildly into the street and shifted into first before coming to a complete stop. He tromped it, and the super-charged V-Eight engine sent his '88 Trans Am fish-tailing down the rain slick street. He ran the first two stop signs while still accelerating. As he turned onto the ramp to the interstate, the wheels screaming terrifically in a slide, the sleek Pontiac slammed into the curb, blowing the left rear tire. Bobby didn't notice until he reached the top of the ramp. He pulled over onto the asphalt berm.

A light autumn mist was falling steadily. In a few moments, his windshield became a matrix of fractured light. The traffic on the interstate tore by, creating a kind of white noise. Bobby Dwyer sat in his Pontiac like a chrysalis in a cocoon. He turned off the engine and tried hard to concentrate. He wasn't crying anymore.

After a while he came to what he thought was a momentous realization. Bobby Dwyer decided that he didn't know how anything worked. That was his problem. He knew some elementary things about the internal combustion engine, but he really didn't know how the car he was sitting in worked. He didn't know how engineers designed and built the highway he was on, the bridges he crossed every day. He didn't know anything at all about chemistry or physics or electricity. And, most importantly, he decided he didn't know anything about women.

Bobby and Ellen had been married a little over two years. They had started dating in high school and everyone knew they would marry. After graduating, Ellen's parents convinced her to go to City Tech to learn how to become a dental hygienist. They also convinced her and the easy-going Bobby to wait at least two years and save a little money before they married. Bobby's uncle, Ted Boyle, landed him a job at Anheuser-Busch, "The Brewery". Ted Boyle had been a master brewer for fifteen years and was a union steward. He arranged a job for his own son, Ted, Jr. and Bobby at the same time in the shipping department and promised them they could eventually work their way up to apprentice brewers.

Ted, Jr., whose nickname was "Sonny", graduated with Bobby and Ellen's high school class and he and Bobby were best friends as well as cousins. Sonny had been the star quarterback on the football team. His easy physical grace, handsome features and a certain wildness created a combination the girls called sexy. He took out several different girls and he and Bobby had often double dated. Before the evening was over, or sometimes just after it had begun, Sonny's date would be down on him in the tiny back seat of Bobby's Trans Am.

When they had been at the Tenth Inning bar, having a few beers without the girls one night, Sonny had said, "I love to watch a girl go down on me. I love the soup sound they make. Especially girls with pretty mouths and little hands, like Ellen's. Know what I mean, Bobby boy?"

A sullen punk named Paulie Husaini was sitting alone at the middle of the bar picking at his teeth with a pocket knife. "I'd rather fight than fuck," he said to no one in particular.

"Nobody would want to fuck a rat face like you, Paulie, except maybe Minnie Mouse," Sonny said. Paulie either had chosen to ignore the remark or he had been too drunk to understand it. He bobbed his head stupidly. A little stream of blood was trickling from his mouth where he had unwittingly cut his gums or his lip. He didn't appear to notice.

Tony "No Gotta" Gatti, the owner, who usually tended bar at night, had eyed the unpredictable Paulie warily. Obviously anxious to keep the peace, he turned to Sonny and said, "The only thing I know is that you're a sick fuck, Boyle. You talk more about your cock and gettin' it sucked than anything. Which makes you what you are: a dick brain."

"Who asked you goombah?" Sonny had said sarcastically.

"Who you callin' goombah, you little mick prick," Tony hissed back in mock anger. "Your name fits you perfectly. You're like a boil on my ass."

"Yeah, yeah, yeah. The dago speaks. But like I was sayin', Bobby, they do love my dick. God bless them everyone."

"Drink your beer, numb nuts." As usual, Tony had to have the last word.

Why hadn't he paid any attention to that stuff: "pretty mouths and little hands like Ellen's." Sonny was the best man at Bobby and Ellen's wedding. But now all kinds of things were going through Bobby's mind. Like the way Ellen would always get on top of him, straddle him while they were making out on double dates with Sonny. Was it so she could see what those girls were doing to Sonny in the back seat?

And when Sonny would come over for supper or to watch a ballgame, Ellen would always sit and watch, too. She didn't know anything about sports and she never watched a game with Bobby alone or with his other friends -- only with Sonny.

"Hey, Ellen, let's you and me leave this nerd-ass couch potato and go to the Rest Well Mo-tel," Sonny had said one night.

"Oh, Sonny, you're so comical," Ellen had replied coyly. "You should be on TV."

But Sonny was his best friend and that kind of good-natured bantering didn't bother Bobby. In fact, it secretly pleased him that Sonny found his wife attractive.

About three months ago, Sonny had stopped coming around. At the time, Bobby thought it was just one of those things that happen. He was married and settled and Sonny was still single. They were just going in different directions. They still talked sports at work (where Sonny was now in the apprenticeship program and Bobby was still on the docks), but they didn't go out drinking with the guys very often any more. But that was just one of those things. He still thought of Sonny as his best friend.

"The dirty motherfucker," Bobby said aloud as he sat in his Trans Am. "The dirty, lousy, motherfucking, shitsack, bastard," he screamed. The rage he felt suddenly stunned him. He could feel his pulse throbbing wildly in his temples. Thinking it would calm him, Bobby decided to fix the flat. He made a terrific effort to do everything methodically. But his hands were still shaking as he tightened the last lug nut.

Bobby drove aimlessly through the familiar streets of South St. Louis. Past Roosevelt High School where he and Ellen had met. Past the Gravois "Show" and the Velvet Freeze where they had gone on their first date. Past the imposing gothic edifice of St. Francis DeSalles Catholic Church where they had been married.

He was beginning to put it all together. As soon as Sonny stopped coming around Ellen had begun to go out at least two or three nights a week for a couple of hours. She would be shopping with Connie Simmons or visiting her aunt at the hospital. And then she would disappear for half a day on Saturday or Sunday. Bobby had trusted her completely. He seldom asked where she was going or where she had been. Jealousy had become her specialty. In the last few months she had begun to accuse *him* of messing around. If he went out for a few beers, she would pump him hard before he left and harder after he got back. He resented it a little because he had been absolutely faithful. But her possessiveness seemed like a sign of love to him. Her insecurity made him feel secure.

What a chump I am, Bobby thought. A world class asshole. He drove by Ellen's parents' house, but no one was home: no lights were burning, the driveway and carport were empty. Then he drove to the apartment complex where Sonny lived. He had no plan and, even though he didn't see Sonny's car in the parking lot, he went up to Sonny's door and began hammering at it with both fists. He didn't stop until the guy in the next apartment opened his door to see what was going on.

Bobby sat in his car outside Sonny's apartment and waited. His brain was reeling and his hands were burning from beating at Sonny's door. He lit a cigarette, the last one in the pack, and tried to formulate a plan. He knew he needed a plan. He wasn't very good at planning. Things just seemed to happen to him. He could follow a path, but he could never formulate a plan. After he finished his cigarette, Bobby drove to the Tenth Inning bar to get another pack. And to get a plan.

It was about seven-thirty when Bobby Dwyer entered the bar. He was given change for the cigarette machine by Tony, who always tended bar on Friday nights. The place was unusually empty. Bobby thought the after work crowd must have already gone home and the late night drinkers had not yet appeared. There were two guys he didn't know playing the bowling machine and Paulie Husaini sat at the far end of the bar playing solitaire and drinking shots of Schnapps, chasing them with draft beer. Tony said Paulie was the only person he ever knew who *always* cheated at solitaire.

"This shitty weather and Connie's party are going to make this a slow night." Tony Gatti was wiping glasses with a soiled towel as Bobby took a seat at a barstool near the door. Tony put a cold bottle of Bud in front of Bobby without being asked.

"Connie's party, that's right, I forgot all about that," Bobby mumbled, as much to himself as to Tony. "Connie's party," he said again distractedly, as he lifted his beer and looked around the almost vacant tavern. Sonny called the place Gatti's Cruddy Penny Arcade...and it did have that atmosphere, with the bowling machine and a juke box against the rear wall, two old-fashioned pinball machines and a video game beside the long bar, as well as a bumper pool table in the middle of the floor. And there was a real oddity next to the cigarette machine by the door: a full sized telephone booth.

The booth was featured in one of the many games Sonny had invented at the Tenth Inning. He called it human-owl. The object was to jump from the top of the cigarette machine to the roof of the telephone booth without using your hands. There was plenty of room, since the original tin ceiling in the turn-of-the-century neighborhood bar was at least fourteen feet high. But Sonny was the only one who had ever done it.

He also had made up human-alligator... crawling down the length of the bar on your belly, commando style. The object of that game was to see how few drinks you would knock over during the trip.

But the most daring game Sonny had ever devised was called human bowling ball. He would set up two tables in front of the bowling machine. And then, after taking a running start, the contestant would dive over the tables and slide down the waxed surface of the bowling machine far enough to reach the brackets which released the electronically triggered pins. You had to be real drunk to play human bowling ball against Sonny.

Thinking of all the good times he had had with Sonny in the Tenth Inning, it suddenly dawned on Bobby that not only had he lost his wife, he was losing his best friend, too. A wave of conflicting emotions surged through him, leaving him more confused than ever.

"Hey Bobby," Tony was saying. "See those two guys bowlin'? They been here maybe two, three hours. When they first come in they order Ca-ronas." Tony lifted his chin to show his disdain. Bobby thought he looked like Mussolini when he made that kind of gesture. Tony had the same square face, jutting jaw and full lower lip Bobby had seen in old newsreels of *Il Duce* on cable TV.

"Fuckin' Ca-ronas. I tell them: Look, I got Bud, I got Busch, I got Mich, I even got Bud Light and Mich Light-- and for you, maybe even Mich Dry... but I ain't got no fuckin' Ca-ronas. No gotta, *capish?* These guys must be from the fuckin' moon. They come into a bar a block from *The Brewery* and order a spic beer. Fuckin' Ca-ronas. Can you believe it? Wise guys."

A few older men from the neighborhood came in within a few minutes of one another and sat at the bar. While Tony waited on them, Bobby finished his beer, lit a cigarette and suddenly, feeling lost and alone, covered his face with his hands for a moment.

"Dwyer. Bobby Dwyer. You look like you need a *real* drink." Paulie Husaini pulled the stool next to Bobby's a little closer and sat down. "Hey Tony, give my high school buddy here a shot of Schnapps. He don't look so good. And bring me one, too." Bobby looked into Paulie's pock-marked face. Sonny called him "The Rat".

And he did look like a rat. His dark, shifty eyes were close together, almost on top of the hook in his Semitic nose. He had a small, tight mouth which barely opened when he spoke. Paulie would have graduated high school with Bobby's class, but he had been kicked out when the cops found a sapper and a snub-nosed .38 in his locker during a routine check. He became a go-fer and a petty enforcer for the Mafia-style Syrian families which controlled several precincts in South St. Louis. They had elected three aldermen, including Paulie's uncle, George Husaini, and were into whores and gambling and extortion on the Southside. But they also controlled several construction unions. And St. Louis was a union town.

"Where's that fuckin' wise mouth Boyle? I thought yous two was

Siamese." Paulie threw back his shot in one gulp. "I never could figure yous guys as asshole buddies. You don't say shit, you got a mouthful and that fuckin' Boyle always yappin' his jaw. It's gonna get him in trouble some day."

"The fucker just ran off with my wife," Bobby said quietly as he lifted his shot glass.

"Say what?"

Bobby was sorry he had said it. Paulie Husaini was one of the few people he didn't like. He was a punk and a troublemaker. But Bobby found himself with a real need to talk about his problem. Even Paulie would do for that. "The fucker ran off with my wife tonight," he said again, trying to speak evenly, but his voice cracked.

"You're serious, ain't you? Mmm, mmm, mmm. The fuckin' weasel run's off with his best buddy's wife. I knew he was a low-life motherfucker. And him with the nerve to call *me* The Rat." Paulie's already squinty eyes narrowed as he spat out those last words. "So what're you gonna do about it?"

"I don't know," Bobby said truthfully, in a voice just above a whisper.

"Well, I know what I'd do. I'd blow his fuckin' head off. Then I'd cut off his fuckin' nuts and stuff 'em in his smart-assed mouth. I'd do it in front of her. And then I'd waste her, too. I'd waste the both of 'em, if it was me." Paulie ordered another round of shots with Budweiser chasers.

Bobby, who hardly ever drank more than four or five beers in a night, threw back the shot and chugged half a bottle of beer to chase it down. He felt the warmth of the liquor's effect spread through his body, into his legs and arms. It calmed him. "That's not my style, Paulie. You know that."

"It ain't your style, huh? Well, when's the last time somebody ran off with your wife? It's like my uncle says: `Drastic things sometime call for drastic measures.' And he didn't get to be no alderman by bein' no dumb-ass."

Bobby didn't say anything. He finished his beer and Paulie ordered another round. "You okay, Bobby?" Tony asked when he delivered the drinks. "Since when do you drink Schapps and perchasers?" Tony glanced at Paulie, but it was clear he didn't want to raise the issue with a Syrian enforcer. Even a small time punk like Paulie Husaini.

"Bobby's okay. Paulie's takin' care of him. You take your guinea ass back to those old farts down the bar."

"I'm okay, Tony," Bobby said, although he was beginning to feel light-headed. "Tonight I can take care of myself." Tony walked to the other end of the bar shaking his head.

"Fuckin' 'A' you can. And you can take care of whoever else needs took care of, too." Paulie picked up Bobby's pack of Marlboros, shook one out and lit it.

Bobby drank the next round more slowly, sipping at the Schnapps, but still gulping the beer. He lit another cigarette although he had one still burning in the ashtray.

"So, I heard you and Tony talkin' about a party at Connie's," Paulie said. "Connie Simmons?" Bobby nodded. "That's where they are, ain't it? Yeah, I'll bet you go there and you'll find Sonny and Ellen. Together." Bobby closed his eyes and nodded slowly. He felt a wave of nausea travel up from the pit of his stomach.

"Come on out to my car and let me show you something," Paulie said. "Come on." Paulie slapped some bills onto the bar and zipped up his nylon wind-breaker. Bobby got up mechanically and let himself be led out the door.

The mist had turned into a freezing rain. The bite from the rain and an unseasonably cold October breeze woke Bobby from his stupor as they trotted across the street to Paulie's red '92 Corvette.

Paulie reached under his seat and pulled out what looked like a bunch of oily rags wrapped with two large rubber bands. He put the package on the console between the bucket seats. Without saying a word, he removed the rubber bands and unwrapped the bundle, revealing three individually wrapped objects. He unwrapped the smallest first. "This is a .32. A personal favorite," Paulie said as he picked up the shiny, well-oiled weapon. He turned it over in his hands carefully, almost lovingly. "A very nice piece at close range." He put it down and unwrapped the second pistol. "This is a .38 police special. It's got more range, more accuracy but it's still easy to conceal on an individual's person." Paulie lapsed into the jargon he had undoubtedly heard in police stations and courts of law. He handed the pistol to Bobby, holding the barrel so Bobby could grasp the grip. Bobby took it without thinking.

"You never held a weapon before, have you?" Paulie asked with a hint of surprise.

"Yes, I have," Bobby said absently, thinking about the time he and Sonny had found a gun behind a pile of debris in a vacant lot. It was wrapped in a big red bandana along with six bullets. They were twelve or thirteen years old and neither he nor Sonny knew the caliber of the pistol. It had a pearl handle, or what looked like a pearl handle, and it was a dull blue-steel color.

Bobby remembered how they had ridden their bicycles the seventeen miles out to Jefferson Barracks, an old abandoned Army installation situated on a bluff overlooking the Mississippi River, to fire their dangerous new possession.

They had climbed down the bluff and over some railroad tracks to the levy where Sonny had loaded the pistol. He let Bobby have the first shot. Bobby shot at a log floating down the swift current of the river and missed, kicking up a spray of murky water. Sonny then shot at the same log and nicked it. As Bobby shouted in triumph, Sonny had suddenly jerked the pistol up and fired two shots rapidly toward the traffic streaming across the Jefferson Barracks Bridge about a quarter of a mile downriver.

Bobby had been stunned. He told Sonny he was a crazy son of a bitch. Then Sonny, saying, "You think I'm crazy, huh?", pointed the gun at Bobby for an instant. And almost in the same motion he did something Bobby could remember as vividly as if it had happened yesterday. Sonny had put the gun up beside his own blonde temple with a wild look in his eyes and a strange sadistic grin on his handsome young face. Just as he squeezed the trigger, he had jerked the gun away from his head, sending the bullet into the air.

Bobby was stupefied as Sonny handed him the pistol so he could take the last shot. A large black bird scavenging on the river bank suddenly lifted into the air in a flutter of furious motion. Bobby, who was still in a state of shock and who was feeling a rage he couldn't understand, swung the gun to a position just ahead of the bird's line of flight, and, without really aiming, squeezed the trigger. The bullet had struck the bird in the head and in a shower of blood and tissue the stricken creature had plummeted to the muddy river waters. Horrified, Bobby had flung the gun as far as he could into the river, much to Sonny's dismay.

Now, as he held the pistol in Paulie's fire-engine red Corvette, Bobby began to feel the same rage he had felt on that river bank. He felt as though the rage was being transmitted to him by the weapon. A lethal weapon. He felt the power and the horror of what that term implied: lethal weapon. Holding this compact, wooden-handled blue steel police special was filling him with an unspeakable and terrible anger. His heart raced and perspiration drenched the underarms of his workshirt and his denim jacket and beaded on his forehead.

Paulie had unwrapped the third bundle. "This is the ultimate handgun; your fabled .44 Magnum. Dirty Harry's weapon of choice. This will blow the back of a man's head off from 100 yards. Ain't it a beauty, Bobby?" He held up the long-barreled polished silver pistol. It gleamed as it caught the beam from the headlights of a passing car. "It's too heavy and too hard to conceal to carry on an individual's person. And that's a cryin' shame." Paulie shook his head and sighed dramatically as he methodically rewrapped the .44. After rewrapping the .32 and stuffing the bundle back beneath his seat, he reached behind him under his jacket and pulled out another weapon. "This is what I carry on my person. Nine millimeter. I even sleep with it in my shorts." He smiled and paused for a moment. "You seem to like that thirty-eight. I'll tell you what. I'm gonna make you a present of it. It's yours." Paulie clapped his hand on Bobby's shoulder and leaned toward him conspiratorially as he lowered his voice. "Now since you told me your troubles, I feel like you're my friend and that I can trust you. I'm gonna tell you a little story that involves a .38." Paulie looked earnestly into Bobby's eyes.

"A lot of guys, includin' your ex-pal Sonny, think I'm a two-bit punk. All show and no go. Well, they're wrong. You know that dago Carmine Mancusso who got it in the parking lot at Little Italy? That was me, the real Paulie Husaini. He was a squealer. Opened his mouth up about the way the families was investin' the pension fund for the steamfitter's union. So me an' another guy took him out. There was supposed to be three of us but this one asshole chickened out. There's nothin' I hate worst than a chickenshit. I ain't gonna tell you the guy's name who did the job with me for your own protection." Paulie smiled and bummed another cigarette from the mesmerized Bobby.

"Carmine comes out of the bar an' I pop him. One. Two. Both in the belly. He falls against that wood fence. Then we go up to him and he's still makin' gurglin' sounds and twitchin', but his eyes are already rolled up in his head. This other guy takes my .38 and puts it in Carmine's liver lip mouth and shuts him up for good. You shoulda seen that fat goombah's brains splatter against that fence. Then we drive to the middle of the Eads Bridge and I put that .38 to sleep at the bottom of the Mississip'." Paulie cracked the window open just enough to flick his cigarette onto the street.

"So what do you think I get for that piece of work?" Paulie didn't wait for a reply. "You're sittin' in it. My uncle gives me this nice Corvette, useta belong to his daughter. He buys her a new one. Maybe it shoulda been the other way around. But I ain't complainin'. A few hours work and I turn my '84 Buick LeSabre into a '92 'vette with all the extras."

Bobby had the strange sensation that Paulie was far away, even though he could feel and smell his pungent alcohol and cigarette tainted breath filling the cockpit-like interior of the compact sports car. He also felt a sense of pity for the ugly and dangerous creature Paulie had become. The newspaper account of Carmine Mancusso's murder Bobby had read said the victim had been shot in the back.

"You know I could be wrong about Sonny," Bobby said. "Ellen left a note and she didn't say anything about Sonny. She just said she was leaving. Said she had to find herself."

"Women don't run off by themself," Paulie said. "So who else would she run off wit'?"

"I don't know." Bobby was beginning to feel confused again. The liquor and the tension had combined to give him a headache. He reached up to rub his temples and realized he was still holding the thirty-eight.

Paulie started the engine and reached across Bobby to open the glove compartment. He took out a silver flask, swallowed a mouthful and handed it to Bobby. Without thinking, Bobby took a swallow and felt a sudden surge of warmth from the Schnapps. "Where does Connie live?" Paulie asked.

"On Eighteenth Street over by Lafayette Park." Bobby gulped down another swallow of the liquor and felt a sudden calmness and a deep sense of resolve. He had a plan and he was about to act upon that plan. He handed the flask to Paulie and stuffed the .38 into the front waistband of his iron-gray work pants.

Although the four or five square blocks which comprised the Lafayette Park district were surrounded by a deteriorating housing project, most of the old brick mansions and rowhouses in the area had been renovated. Connie Simmons lived with two roommates in a rowhouse which had been converted into a two-story townhouse apartment. The brick was painted light blue and the ornate stonework under the eaves, above the windows and around the arched front doorway created a handsome contrast.

The smell of marijuana greeted Bobby and Paulie as they reached the top of the stairs to the front stoop. Eddie Wiggins and Joe Patterson were standing in the recessed entrance passing the joint between them.

"What d'ya say, Bobby," Eddie said, obviously delighted to see his old high school pal. "Fuckin' Connie won't let us smoke no dope in her crib. She says the smell gets in the drapes and carpet and shit and her old lady smells it when she comes over and gives her a ration of shit for bein' a dope head. Where's Ellen?"

"It don't make no sense to me," Joe broke in. "Fuckin' beer and whiskey gets spilled all over everything, but that's okay. It don't make no sense, does it Bobby?"

"You guys seen Sonny Boyle?" Paulie asked tersely.

"I seen him in the kitchen a few minutes ago talkin' to Bernie Petrosky," Eddie said. "You're Paulie Husaini, ain't ya? I remember you from Miss Beck's Home Room in high school. She was always on your ass. I'm Eddie Wiggins." Paulie nodded and brushed past him to the front door, steering Bobby in front of him with his body. "Hey Bobby," Eddie yelled after them. "You won't recognize Bernie if you ain't seen him since high school. He goes maybe 240, 250. Looks like the fuckin' Goodyear blimp."

Bobby could feel the sharp butt of the pistol against his stomach with each step he took. He half-heartedly acknowledged the greetings from the people he knew as he made his way down the hall to the kitchen. He could feel the stolid weight of the short but stocky Paulie shadowing him, pressing him forward without actually touching him.

Bobby saw Sonny in the corner of the kitchen still talking to Bernie Petrosky. Seeing Sonny's animated face smiling in jovial conversation enraged Bobby. He pulled the pistol as he crossed the room and pointed it at Sonny's head.

"What's this, cops and robbers?" Sonny said as he pushed Bobby's arm away from his face.

"Where's Ellen, you cocksucker?" Bobby watched Sonny's face, but couldn't read what was going on is his eyes or his expression.

"You tell me where she is." Sonny seemed perplexed, but Bobby thought he was making a terrific effort to remain calm. He didn't look afraid.

"I can't believe you'd do this to me, Sonny. Why would you do this to me?" Bobby's voice cracked as his rage became tempered by confusion. He felt his eyes filling with tears.

Bobby was surprised and frightened by the agitation in Paulie's eyes as they darted from his face to Sonny's. Suddenly Paulie pulled out his nine millimeter pistol. "Pop him," Paulie hissed. "Cut the crap and pop the motherfucker, Bobby."

"You gonna shoot me, Bobby?" Sonny asked calmly. "Go ahead, shoot me."

"Pop him, you chickenshit motherfucker. I came here to shoot somebody." Paulie's eyes were now glazed in a kind of wild fury Bobby had never seen before.

Bobby began to cry silent, hot tears as he brought his gun down from Sonny's face. He stepped back and let his hand drop. He felt tired, confused and ashamed. He looked up toward Paulie and saw with amazing clarity, as though it were in slow motion, the barrel of the nine millimeter pistol turn in his direction. He heard the double click as Paulie pulled the trigger. But Bobby Dwyer didn't hear the report... the bullet had already exploded in his brain.

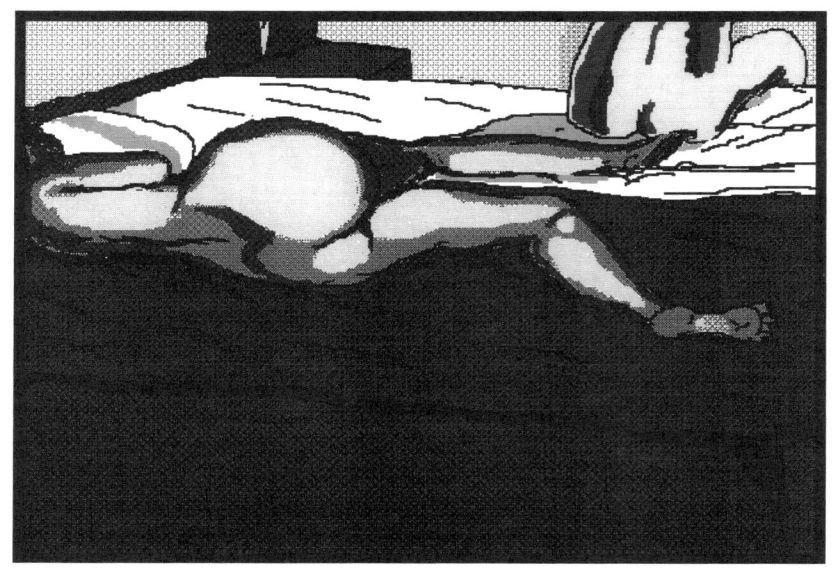

WHY DO BIRDS SING?

I sat naked on the edge of our king size waterbed. My wife Carolyn and I had just made love. We used to have great sex in the morning after the kids had left for school. Now, more often than not, we had what I thought of as maintenance sex; a kind of mutual masturbation. It was better than nothing, but it was a mystery to me how we had both come to accept this kind of mechanical sex life.

A lot of things were becoming a mystery to me. One of these was Carolyn's sudden obsession with the size of her ass. I watched her as she stood naked in front of the long mirror hanging on the door to our walk-in closet. She grabbed the flesh at the back of her thighs and made a grotesque parody of what she seemed to think was her worst feature.

I knew she was unhappy. And I also knew it would only be a matter of time before she would try to make me just as unhappy. It was a kind of game we had begun to play. I sometimes wondered if the essence of our marriage was this continuing attempt to control each others emotions in a negative way. It was one of the things that had led to the end of my first marriage.

The truth was I thought Carolyn was beautiful. But I was certain if I told her that, she would think I was putting her on. When she was in a funk, anything I said could be turned around in a hurtful way. Don't get me wrong, she wasn't beautiful like a model. She was beautiful like the girl next door; with freckles and a slight gap between her front teeth and a nose too small for her face. I liked everything about her body; even her bony knees and extra long second toes.

I watched her. She was the mother of my children, and once had been the light of my life. My first marriage was a result of lust and an unwanted pregnancy. We were just kids, both nineteen. We had just started to really know each other when the baby miscarried. It turned out we didn't like each other much. We argued for six months before we split for good.

But it was different with Carolyn. She was my boss's daughter. We dated for two years before we were married, just like in a Doris Day movie. She was fifteen years younger than I, but she was bright and she could be a lot of fun. And she could be terrific in bed. She had a great ass and she knew how to use it when she felt good about herself.

"Liposuction," Carolyn said as she pursed her lips and sucked in her cheeks. "It's the only answer. Wendy Pearson says that Jeff Robertson is actually a competent plastic surgeon. Even if he does feel up his patients." She chuckled as she turned to face me. "I weigh 110 pounds and my ass is about to fall down to my knees."

"Poor baby," I said as I walked toward the bathroom.

"You don't understand anything, Michael."

I turned on the shower and stepped back in to the bedroom. "This is what I understand. I know if I brought ten people in here and asked them, "Is this woman fat? Is she grotesque? Is her ass hanging down to her knees?' All ten would say, 'Are you crazy? She is a rail. She is a fucking knockout.'"

"See, that's exactly what you don't understand. I don't care what ten people or ten thousand people would say about my ass. The important thing is how *I feel* about my ass. And I feel as though my ass is about to fall down to my knees."

"And your teeth are crooked."

"Yes my teeth *are* crooked." She pulled down her lower lip to show me her bottom teeth. "Look how these three teeth overlap. I need braces."

"When you smile, no one even sees your bottom teeth. You have gorgeous teeth," I said lamely.

"They're yellow. Permanently stained," she said petulantly. "I'm going to have them bleached or capped, and I'm going to have braces put on the bottom ones. Wendy says she knows a dentist in Clayton who is fabulous."

"And what about your tits? Don't you want a tit-job like Wendy's?" I stepped into the shower.

"Now that's where I draw the line," she shouted so she could be heard over the blast of water. "I think big tits look ridiculous on a small person."

She was quiet for a moment and then she pulled back the shower curtain and said, "Do you think my tits are too small?"

"They're perfect," I said. "Just like ripe, Jonathan apples. Unbelievably pert for a woman your age."

"What do you mean by that smart-assed remark? I'm only thirty-two." She closed the shower curtain abruptly.

"Jesus this is a stupid conversation," I said as I soaped myself vigorously, the hot water pounding pleasurably on my shoulders and back. After I finished my shower and dried myself thoroughly, I turned on my hair dryer. Carolyn sat at her vanity in the bedroom and mumbled something I couldn't hear over the sound of the dryer. I turned it off.

"Why do you always start a conversation when I'm drying my hair?"

"Why do you always start drying your hair when I'm talking to you?"

"Right," I said. "What is it?"

"We're going to the Pearson's tonight for cocktails and a cookout. You have to take Richie to baseball practice at six because I have a hair appointment, and I'll drop Melanie off at mother's. You pick up the babysitter at seven-thirty."

"Anything else?" I asked, more than a little peeved by the tone of her voice, matter-of-factly ordering me around.

"Yes," she said. "Pete has this friend who is visiting from England. He's some kind of semi-famous playwright or something. Anyway, it's important to them."

"Will the Antresians be there?" I asked.

"Of course they'll be there. Do you think Susan would miss a chance to meet a celebrity? I hope you and Don have enough graciousness not to turn on the TV and watch the Card's game all night," Carolyn said. "And please wear a tie."

"Why should I wear a tie? I have to wear a tie all day at work. I hate ties and you know it."

"See, you just want to start a fight. It's a simple request. Please wear a tie. All the other men will be wearing ties. Please wear a tie. But no, not you. You won't even make a simple, minor concession for me, will you? You'd think I was asking you to cut off your goddamn arm."

"I don't like to wear ties to cookouts."

"Go fuck yourself then."

I turned the hair dryer back on and finished combing my hair. As I was shaving, she slammed a few doors while getting dressed and took our terrier (she had named Boodles) for his morning walk. I gulped down a cup of instant coffee and left for work before she was back.

It was a spectacular morning. A bright red cardinal and a brilliant blue jay swooped in the river birches near our driveway, chirping their spring songs. I rolled down all the electrically controlled windows and opened the moon roof on the Buick Electra I was using. It was one of the perks of being the general manager of a new car dealership. I turned up the radio as I reached Interstate 55. The nine o'clock news gave way to a fast-talking rap-style McDonald's commercial, and then my morning companion came on one of the Oldies stations, WWFO.

"Hey, Mommio— ho, Daddio. This is Billy Bishop on your raddio. And I'm back with my stacks of wax and grooves sayin' ooo pop a do and a how do you do— eee tiddle eee ock (thump, thump) let's rock. Yes, my darlings, this is your blast from the past, WWFO, Way Way Far Out. And Billy's got little Frankie Lyman and the Teenagers ready for you to start off this rockin' good morning. It's springtime and here's Frankie with, 'Why Do Fools Fall in Love?'"

And Frankie Lyman began to sing in his high falsetto voice the song which had a special significance to me. It was the tune that a curly-haired fifteen year-old named June Carlson and I called "our" song in 1956. I hummed the first few bars and then remembered the words to the second verse and sang along: "Why do birds sing so gay,/and lovers await the break of day./Why do they fall in love?" I let myself get caught up in the song, immersed in the blatant and corny nostalgia of the moment. I felt ridiculously happy and liberated.

June Carlson had always worn these baggy sweaters and blouses in an era when tight fitting cashmeres had been the norm. She introduced me to the concept of "surprisers". One night I had fumbled to unhook the back of her bra in my Dad's 1955 Ford Fairlane. And when I had finally succeeded, I lifted up her sweater and saw these two huge and wonderfully symmetrical breasts with the biggest, pinkest nipples I had ever seen. They were about the size of "I Like Ike" campaign buttons. I was stunned by the sheer enormity and purity of those unexpected breasts. They were at least twice as big as I had imagined. I was so awestruck I just buried my head in their abundance and held on to her in a profound and unequalled gratitude.

"Thank you Jesus," I had muttered, completely convinced that not only was there a God, but that He had chosen to smile upon me in all His beatitude that hot summer night. June, of course, didn't know what the fuss was all about, and the intensity of my emotion seemed to frighten her. That was as far as I ever got with her, but I remember singing "O Holy Night" reverently and fervently as I drove home after dropping her off that night.

Lost in my reverie, I almost missed my exit and had to dart across two lanes of the late morning traffic to get on the off ramp to Lindbergh Road. As I pulled onto the new car lot, a young family was standing next to a new two-door Buick Reatta. The slender, bearded father, dressed in corduroys and a striped rugby shirt, was shading his eyes and peering into the window on the driver's side. His very pregnant wife was standing beside him trying to quiet the squalling toddler she was holding by forcing a baby bottle into it's uncooperative mouth.

I drove to the employee's parking area on the left side of the new car showroom. That's when I noticed Donilo Antresian, Hoffmeister Nissan-Buick's top salesman and my long-time friend and neighbor. He was leaning nonchalantly against a mid-size Buick Century station wagon. Dressed in a stylish dark gray Italian-made suit (he had told me it was 75% silk and 25% linen), a dazzling white shirt with a stiff starched collar, a $250 pair of Bally cordovan shoes and a subtly patterned maroon on maroon tie with matching breast pocket handkerchief, Antresian looked like an Italian don— or maybe a caricature of the dishonest assholes car salesmen are supposed to be. A direct descendent of ancient Anatolian rug merchants, Antresian had chosen the perfect modern equivalent of that profession; seller of brand new magic carpets made of steel and chrome and fiberglass and rubber.

"Get away from that car," Antresian shouted at the family eyeing the Reatta. "That car is not for you. Come over here a minute."

The young man squinted at him from across the lot forty yards away, shielding his eyes from the low but already bright morning sun. I decided to sit in my car parked only fifty feet from where Antresian was standing to see how he would work the sale.

"Come on over here," Antresian commanded like a firm, yet kindly father. He had not altered his posture and still leaned against the front fender of the dark blue wagon, his legs crossed at the ankles. The young father took a few uncertain steps toward Antresian, followed by his wife, still struggling with her fussing child.

When they reached him, Donilo sprang forward and thrust out his right hand. "Don Antresian, nice to see ya."

"Vic Damon," the father said as he shook Antresian's hand weakly.

"Vic Damone. Then this must be Edie Gormé," Antresian said as he abruptly dropped the man's hand and extended his own to the mother. She deposited the toddler expertly on to her left hip and firmly shook Donilo's hand.

"Charlotte," she said. "Charlotte Whittington-Damon."

"It's a pleasure to meet ya. Two famous singers." Donilo shook his head as though in true wonderment.

"Vic, take these keys," Donilo said as he thrust out his left hand and dangled a set of keys about chest high. The young father reached for the keys instinctively just as Donilo let them drop. They clattered on the paved lot. Vic bent down to retrieve them.

"See, Vic and Edie, this is the car for you. You've already got one beautiful kid looks like he should be in a diaper commercial and another one in the oven. Did you see the back area in that Reatta? It won't do. You fold up a stroller and put it back there, where you gonna put the babies? Drive this," Donilo said as he stepped back and made a sweeping gesture toward the wagon. "Take this baby for a spin. Go over to the shopping mall. Take her down the interstate. Get in."

"You're moving a little fast here, aren't you, Don? You did say your name was Don didn't you?", the young man asked.

"Drive the car, Vic," Donilo said.

"Well, there are a few things I'd like to ask you first, if you don't mind." A little peevishness began to creep into Vic's voice. Charlotte compressed her lips in a show of solidarity.

"Drive the car, Vic."

"How do you know we want a station wagon, which we don't. And, if we did, how do you now we would want this one?" Vic asked rhetorically.

"Drive the car, Vic."

"What's the sticker price?" Vic asked.

Donilo moved over in front of the rear window on the driver's side where the sticker was posted. "Drive the car, Vic. Take her anywhere you like for the rest of the morning. Here's a tape of the *Big Chill* sound track. Pop it in the quad stereo sound system and take the wagon for a spin. The tape is yours if you buy from me or not. *Gratis.*"

"Is it a six cylinder or a V-eight?" Vic moved toward the hood and began to look over the gleaming new wagon for the first time with some interest.

"Drive the car, Vic." And with that Donilo took a pair of Carrera sunglasses from his inside jacket pocket, put them on methodically, turned his back and walked away from the bewildered young family. Antresian didn't look back as he walked into the showroom and disappeared behind a partition leading to the snack area.

"It's not bad is it, Charlotte?" Vic said. "Hell, let's take it for a ride. What've we got to lose?"

Charlotte shrugged her shoulders and said, "He's crude and rude." But she opened the door to the wagon. Donilo had placed a baby seat on the passenger side. Charlotte strapped in the toddler, put him in the back seat and they drove off the lot, turning left onto Lindbergh toward the South County Shopping Mall and Interstate 55.

"Steve Lawrence," I said as I caught up with Donilo. He was pouring himself a cup of coffee.

"Steve Lawrence, what?" Donilo asked.

"Steve Lawrence was Edie Gormé's husband. He was a singer and an alcoholic," I said. As soon as I said "alcoholic" I realized that is the way Carolyn would describe someone: with an unnecessary and even nonessential piece of information.

"Who gives a fuck. That scraggly-bearded little mooch can't find his ass with both hands. What does he know from Vic Damone, Steve Lawrence or Edie Gormé? We're talkin' babies, Mikey. But I'll bet you fifty green ones they buy that wagon if Charlotte don't queer the deal."

"She thinks you're crude. Crude and rude. She said that when you walked away," I said, smiling.

"On his death bed my father told me three things about women.

One— never get involved with a woman whose mouth makes a straight line when she's pissed. Strike one. Two— never get involved with a woman with two last names. Strike two. Three— Make sure you marry a woman with small hands. It'll make your dick look bigger. Charlotte's hands are bigger than Dr. J's and her feet are bigger than Jackie Kennedy's. Strike three and she's out." Donilo popped two pills in his mouth and swallowed a half a cup of coffee in one gulp.

"Your father died when you were three."

"I was smart for my age. He thought I could handle it." Donilo laughed and then clutched at his stomach. "This fuckin' ulcer's killing me, Mikey."

As Donilo bent over in exaggerated pain, Stan "Whitey" Kurowski, our service manager came in to the snack room. "Whitey" had dark brown hair. His nickname was a result of having the same last name as the Whitey Kurowski who played for the St. Louis Cardinals baseball team in the '40s.

"Hey Whitey," Donilo said. "Do you know why they put a pile a shit in the corner at Polish weddings?"

"Go fuck yourself up the ass with a gear shift, greaseball," Kurowski said evenly.

"To keep the flies off the bride."

Kurowski, who was as big as an NFL tackle, chased Donilo around the room, swatting at him with the sheaf of green repair orders he had in his hand. Donilo had told a Polish joke every day for about two weeks and Kurowski always chased him around the room for a few seconds until they both ran out of breath. He loved Antresian though. Donilo was the only one who would stick up for the service department with a customer. All the other salesmen folded at the first sign of discontent, making Kurowski's life miserable. He downed his Coke in one long swallow as Donilo shook his head in amazement.

"This goddamn Polack drinks six Cokes by ten o'clock in the morning. Fuckin' cast iron stomach. I drink one lousy cup a coffee, and it eats a hole in my belly the size of a quarter."

Kurowski put his arm around Donilo's shoulder and whispered with phony menace, "I could do us both a favor and crack your ugly Armenian head open like a walnut." He lifted a leg, farted loudly and left.

"Donilo," I said, "I got some bad news for you on this Tommy

Peter's deal. G.M.A.C. won't finance the car. The kid is bad pay."

"Come on, Mike, that's a rock solid deal. I know the kid's old man and uncle. Take it to the Nazi and we can finance it ourselves. The pimply-faced little fucker misses one payment I go to his house, tear his heart out, bring it here and eat it in front of Hoffmeister. On my mother's head."

"Donilo, Donilo. Who you talkin' to? I'm not some bimbo at Bugazzi's bar. This is your grade school buddy, Mike Webster. Best man at your wedding. Godfather to your children. This deal won't fly." I handed him the contract.

"Will you take it to Hoffmeister if I get the kid's old man to co-sign?"

"That I will do."

"You're a hard man, Michael. That's why you're the boss and I'm still a schlepper." Donilo folded up the contract and put it in his back pocket. "I sold five cars this week; six if Vic and Edie come through. I'm takin' the afternoon off. Why don't you come over to the track with me? I got a tip on a thirty to one shot, Bootin' 'n Scootin', in the third at Fairmont. The number two horse, Lena's Lover, is supposed to be a mortal lock at even money, but my bookie tells me his head will be pointed straight at the heavens from the minute he reaches the top of the stretch. Bootin' 'n Scootin' is a closer. Wanna go, Mikey?"

"Naw, I've got too much paperwork to do."

"Okay, I'll watch the ponies and you drive your desk."

And I felt a little envy as Donilo shrugged his shoulders in a "too bad" gesture and walked out to the showroom.

Donilo had helped me get my first job as a used car salesman. I had worked as a carpenter's apprentice after I married my first wife. Then I had gone to St. Louis Community College for a couple of semesters after the divorce, but I was never a great student in high school and I didn't have enough discipline to study at the college level. So I went to work for McCarthy Ford, and it turned out I was a pretty good salesman. Not as good as Donilo, of course, but I was thorough, and I followed through, and I did all the paperwork right.

Don McCarthy had made me Used Car Sales Manager after only eight months. I had a lot of drive and ambition in those days and I guess he saw that in me. So did Hoffmeister. He had stolen me away from McCarthy thirteen years ago by making me New Car Manager of his Buick dealership. Then, after I married his daughter, he had promoted me to General Manager. That's when I returned the favor and hired Donilo.

As I walked by Hoffmeister's office to get to my own, the old man looked up from the newspaper he was reading and motioned for me to come in. He had this big window in his office, almost floor to ceiling, so he could watch the showroom. He would time the salesmen with a stopwatch. It was his firm belief that any salesman who talked to a customer for more than two minutes without moving him toward a car was talking himself out of a sale.

"Whose idea was this ad, takes up almost a whole page and ain't even in the new car section," he said without looking up or taking the long and fat unlit Havana cigar out of his mouth.

"It was the ad agency's idea, but I approved it. You remember I asked you if I could spend the money over and above the co-op for a special ad," I said. He had me on the defense.

"I know what you asked." He looked up and adjusted his bifocals so he could see over them and stare me in the eye. "But why would you make an ad that takes up a whole page and only has a picture of one Jap car in it?"

"The Agency thought if we put this ad for the Nissan Infiniti in the Business section, we'd attract a lot of new lookers. Then once we get them in the showroom we could sell them whatever. I think it was a good idea." I matched his stare for a minute, but I already knew I'd blink first. Nobody could outstare Otto Hoffmeister.

"I been in this business thrity-five years, Michael, and I ain't never seen no newspaper ad like this. You got this big blank page. This picture of a Jap car in the middle. A few words I can't read underneath the picture and then in the corner, so small I can't read it without my bifocals, you got Hoffmeister Nissan-Buick. No address, no phone number. What kind of a newspaper car ad is that?"

I shrugged my shoulders. "A pretty good one, I think."

"What you did here is make a magazine ad, Michael. The Jap agency spends thousands of dollars for bullshit ads like this in Conyousewer magazine and what have you. But we ain't selling no one of a kind Marco Angelos in the *St. Louis Post Dispatch*. You know better than anybody we got almost 500 cars in our inventory and most of them are Buicks. You got to garish up these newspaper ads so the working man, who don't read no Conyousewer magazine, can do a little shopping before he gets here. *Verstahen*, Michael?" He lit his cigar with a gold lighter without moving his eyes from mine. The phone rang before I could answer his question, which was just as well because I didn't know what to say to the fucking hardheaded Kraut anyway.

"Hello, my little Cocoa Puff," Hoffmeister smiled his gap-toothed smile (the first smile I had seen on his face for days), and leaned back in his over-sized executive leather chair. He called Carolyn Cocoa Puff because she had been crazy for that cereal in her early teens. Her mother said she used to eat those sugar-coated little balls by the handful right from the box while she watched TV.

"Why do you get a babysitter. We can watch the *kinders*," Hoffmeister said and then frowned as he listened to his daughter's explanation. "Ah, your mother's always dragging me to that goddamn county club. I don't know why she wants to go there. I can buy and sell half them bastards ten times over and they treat me like a D.P. just off the boat." He listened some more then leaned forward, glanced up at me, and said, " Yeah, he's right here in my office. I'll have Dorothy transfer you to his phone." He listened again and smiled briefly. "Yeah, me too. I'm kookoo for Cocoa Puffs." He pushed the hold button and frowned at me as he crumpled the newspaper into a ball and tossed it into the wastebasket beside his desk. Without saying a word he dismissed me from his office with a motion of his big, bald head.

I had just about had it with the Hoffmeister brand of logic and reason, their firm grasp on absolute truth. Like father, like daughter, I thought as I punched the blinking button on my phone and lifted the receiver, waiting to hear another dose of infinite Hoffmeister wisdom.

"Yeah," I said abruptly.

"What's eating you?"

"Nothing," I lied.

"I forgot to tell you to stop by Dierbourg's and buy a couple of bottles of wine on your way home. We can't go to the Pearson's empty-handed." She was using that same tone of voice that set my teeth on edge earlier. "There's this great new California Chardonnay from Glen Ellen. I think the stuff Wendy and I had at lunch the other day was 1992. It's about eight or nine dollars a bottle. Don't forget."

I started to ask why she didn't have the time to go herself, but she had already hung up. I shuffled some papers around half-heartedly for about an hour, when Dorothy Jenkins, our fiftyish receptionist and secretary, stuck her pleasantly plump face into my doorway to ask if I wanted anything for lunch from Hardee's across the street. Donilo came up behind her and blew into her ear before I could answer. She swatted at him playfully and adjusted her bra. For some reason Donilo seemed to have this effect on most women. He could say or do almost anything that would get most guys a cold shoulder if not a slap in the face. And the women always seemed to start fooling with their hair or their clothes when he stood next to them. He was a born salesman. Even Hoffmeister, who didn't like anything about Donilo, admitted he was the best salesman who had ever worked for him. "He could sell ice to Eskimos, sand to Arabs and shoes to a legless man," Hoffmeister told me one day. "But he's oily, and I don't like oily."

"Last chance," Donilo said to me as he rubbed the back of his hand against Dorothy's blushing cheek. She didn't pull away. "It's Hardees' greaseburgers with Dorothy and the Polack or Bugazzio's pasta *fasole* with me and an afternoon in the sun watching those ponies. The sweet life."

"There's a shipment of Skylarks coming in this afternoon, don't forget," Dorothy said to me with a look of concern. "Don't let this good-for-nothing corrupt you."

"I know, Dorothy," I said, forcing a smile. "I'll have a double with pickles and mustard, some curlycue fries and an apple turnover." I felt as sad as a little boy who was being punished and couldn't go out to play.

"Okay, boss," Donilo said. "I'll see you tonight at Pete's party. The Cards are playing the Cubbies in Chicago. It's on Channel 4. Susan and Carolyn will be all over that Limy actor or whatever the hell he is and we won't even be missed." Donilo blew Dorothy a kiss and started to leave.

"Christ, I almost forgot," Donilo said as he stepped past Dorothy into my office. He reached into the inside pocket of his jacket and pulled out a new sales contract. Dorothy pinched her nose and waved away an imaginary smell as she turned to walk down the hall.

"Vic and Edie came through. I low-balled them. I know they're going to call the other dealers— Hanrahan and Costello and maybe even Gordon in Belleville. That Blue Whale's been on the lot for almost a year, so I figure you can talk the old man out of a bill or a bill and a half so I don't have to take too much of a bath on my commish."

Donilo rolled his eyes and said, "I bet they come back with a coach or a hero. Some know-it-all with a fist full of degrees who fixes Volvos and Saabs. Ah ba da ba da ba, a salesman's life is hell," he said as he folded up the contract and put it back in his inside pocket. Donilo smiled and put his hands out in a supplicant's gesture as he shrugged his shoulders and left.

After I had wolfed down the lukewarm and unsatisfying fast food Dorothy brought us, I slumped down in my chair feeling very lonely. I took a chance that my sister would be home on what had become a beautiful Saturday afternoon and dialed her number.

"Hello."

"Hello, is this Margaret Dugan the kindergarten teacher at Warren Elementary?" I was pretty good at disguising my voice, particularly if I put the receiver under my chin.

"Yes, this is Margaret Dugan.

"Well, this is an obscene phone call: Ka-ka, pee-pee, poo-poo."

Her laugh, which was as delightfully familiar to me as my daughter's sweet innocence, started in small spurts and then burst into breath-robbing guffaws as she tried to say my name. Knowing that I could still make her laugh, as I did when we were children, was immensely satisfying, out of all proportion to the actual fact.

"The Hoffmeister's have got me down again, Maggie," I said, recognizing an unpleasant whine in my voice which I could not suppress.

There are any number of things Maggie could have said to put things in perspective. But what she did say confirmed my wisdom in calling her: "In the immortal words of Patrick Fitzgerald Webster, God rest his soul: `Fuck them Hoffmeisters and the Buicks they rode in on.'"

"I miss dad, and I miss you Maggie. What are you doing tonight?"

"Steve's going to play cards with his buddies from The Brewery, so I guess I'm going to clean behind the refrigerator and read some Proust to punish myself for getting involved with another asshole." It was true that Maggie had bad luck with men.

"Well, according to Carolyn, there'll be a celebrity at the party we're going to tonight at the Pearson's. How would you like to meet a semi-famous playwright from England? An English major like you should find this guy right up her alley."

"I don't want to find anybody up my alley, thank you. Besides I majored in the language not the country, sweetheart. And ever since Dugan took a powder, whenever I hear the word "writer" I reach for my revolver." Maggie's first husband, David Dugan, was a columnist for the now defunct *St. Louis Globe-Democrat*. He left her for a copygirl half his age. "Who's watching the kids?" she asked.

"Carolyn has lined up our regular sitter."

"Forget about a sitter. I'll pay her what she would have made and come over. I'm working on this new computer program for my class and Melanie can give me valuable feedback. I don't know where that kid gets her brains. You sure she's not a foundling?"

"Eat shit and die, little sister." It was my standard line for her relentless sarcasm. "I'll see you at seven-thirty."

"In the immortal words of Patrick Fitzgerald Webster: `When things go wrong, as they sometimes will. When the road your trudging seems all uphill. When the funds are low and the debts are high; and you want to smile, but you have to sigh. "When...'"

"Goodbye, Maggie," I interrupted, but she was still reciting the last line's of our father's favorite corny, poetic homily as I hung up. And I could see his Irish-English horsey face, flushed from too much scotch, a long finger waving back and forth; and the voice, the deep melodious voice giving an air of dignity to even that silly piece of doggerel: "When care is pressing you down a bit, rest if you must, but *never* quit."

II

Thurston Walker, Pete and Wendy's semi-famous British playwright, was a pretty regular guy in a lot of ways. It's always a little annoying when you're prepared to dislike someone on sight and they turn out to be charming and likable. Although he didn't disappoint in the area of the tweeds (even his tie had a herringbone pattern), Walker's clean-shaven face was open and seemed honest and friendly. Even Donilo, who was probably the best phony detector I had ever known, warmed to Walker when he started talking about beer.

"I'm almost ashamed to admit that not one brand of beer in all of England can stand up in flavor and sheer drinkablity to your Budweiser," Walker said to Donilo as we stood on the patio in the Pearson's backyard. As if to emphasize his point, Walker downed a whole bottle of Bud in three or four long swallows without taking it from his lips. "And you say it's brewed here in St. Louis?" Donilo nodded. "Remarkable."

Just as Donilo had predicted, the women were all over Walker. He seemed to be one of those rare men who are as comfortable talking with women as they are with men. He was tall and slim, and although his complexion had apparently been ravaged by some childhood pox, he was handsome enough. Wendy Pearson said she thought he looked like Richard Burton.

"Before or after his interment?" Walker asked with mock solemnity. The women ate it up.

Carolyn seemed particularly smitten. There were about twenty people at the party and as Walker moved from group to group easily joining each conversation, Carolyn followed him like a puppy. I didn't think anything of it because I knew Carolyn needed a lot of attention. Flirting seemed to make her feel alive; and later that night, or the next morning, I could usually reap the benefits of her improved attitude about herself.

After we had eaten, Pete, Donilo and I went down to the lowest level of Pete's tri-level house, down to what Wendy called her Great Room. What I thought was "great" about it was watching baseball on Pete's 42 inch Mitsubishi TV. To my surprise, Walker came down too.

"No doubt about it," Donilo said. "The fucking Japanese make the most reliable cars and the clearest TVs."

"It's because their women all have flat rear ends," Walker said. "It's my flat rear end theory of productivity."

Donilo loved it. "Okay, I'll bite. How come?" he asked smiling from ear to ear.

"Quite simple really. Japanese men don't want to go home to those flat asses, so they labor all night perfecting their autos and telies," Walker said with a straight face. "That's also why you've never heard of a superior telie being manufactured in Zimbabwe."

"Or in Mikey's basement," Donilo said as he and Pete doubled over in laughter. I laughed too.

The Cards were leading the Cubs two to one and were at bat in the top of the seventh when we ran out of beer. Wendy and Carolyn had recaptured poor Walker after the second inning and had taken him back upstairs to the rest of the party. To his credit, Walker seemed genuinely reluctant to leave.

"Who's gonna go get some more Bud?" Pete asked a little sheepishly. "What d'ya say we flip for it. Odd man flies. I buy.

"What are you talking about, Pearson," Donilo said. "You're the fucking host here. You mean to tell me you wanna flip with your honored guests for who's gonna miss two innings of the best game so far this year? Surely you jest."

"Let one of the girls go," I suggested.

"Great idea, Webster," Pete said. He ran upstairs to tell Wendy and was back before the first batter struck out.

The Cardinals hung on to win three to two in regulation. No beer had arrived, but we were too wrapped up in the game to notice. When we went back upstairs, most of the remaining guests were leaving. Carolyn and Walker weren't there.

"Do you think she had a wreck?" Wendy asked. "God I'd feel terrible if she had a wreck. They've been gone almost an hour."

"Carolyn insisted on going," Susan Antresian said. "Thurston said he'd tag along. They were just going down to LeMay Plaza Liquors."

Just then we heard the side door to the kitchen bang open. Carolyn was giggling. We were all standing by the front door. Pete, Wendy, Susan, Donilo and I. The rest of the guests had gone. I walked to the kitchen and Donilo followed me two or three steps behind. No one else spoke or moved.

When Carolyn saw me she seemed to shutter slightly. An involuntary tremor shook her shoulders, her neck, her face. And then she smiled warmly and made a move toward me. Her face was blurred, that out of focus look of the well and soundly fucked I had seen so often and loved so well.

When she was within striking distance, I turned slightly and my fist shot out catching her full on the mouth. I didn't think about it. I can't even remember willing the blow. It just happened. Carolyn fell in a heap against the kitchen cabinets. Her lips were split. She tried to staunch the flow of blood from her mouth with both hands.

"I say ...." Walker began.

"You say nothing." Donilo never lost his head when he was truly angry. He pushed the unresisting Walker out the side door.

And then I was in the car, the beautifully appointed Buick Electra, Donilo was sitting beside me and I was driving the two miles to my house. I now know I could make the trip blindfolded, because I couldn't see a thing. I'm not even sure what I felt beyond a crushing numbness. A terrific inertia. As though I were turning to stone.

Donilo whispered some words to Maggie. The children were upstairs asleep. We sat in my living room. In the exact chairs we had sat in the night my father had died three years before. Maggie turned out the lights. I think it was Donilo who began the rocking motion. We rocked and rocked. The only sound I remember hearing was the song of the nightbirds. A cluster of whippoorwills, I think. They sang and sang.

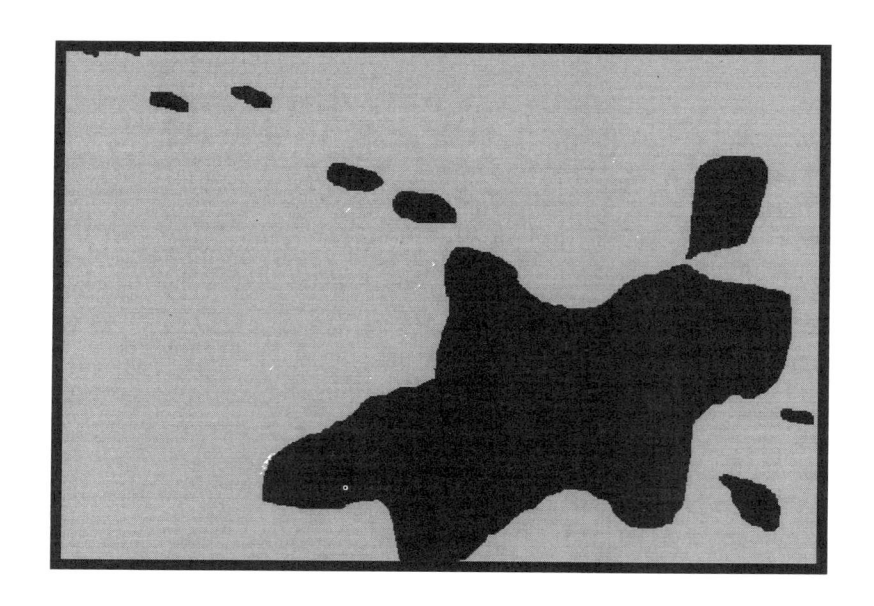

KILLER KARDONOWAY

Michael Kardonoway became "Killer" Kardonoway on a hot, humid August afternoon in 1954. He and five other boys were playing stickball with a rubber ball and a broom stick on Menard Street in South St. Louis. An ancient tom cat, apparently stupefied by the heat, left the shelter of the shade beneath a curbside oak and ambled into the path of a battered '48 Chevy.

The car hit the brown and white cat a glancing blow, but with sufficient force to knock it back onto the sidewalk in front of Michael's house. The driver didn't stop despite the jeering of the boys as he sped through their improvised playing field.

The big cat's head was lying in a pool of blood when the boys reached it. But it wasn't dead. It was moaning; making a low, soft, steady, eerily human sound. Michael Kardonoway recognized the sound. His mother made the same sound after being struck by his father in a drunken rage.

"We've got to do something," Michael said, unnerved as much by the sound as by the wretched suffering of the cat.

"We could call the Humane Society," Ronnie Crawford suggested. "They'll put him to sleep."

"Hell, the Humane Society won't come down here for a stinking old tom cat," Ronnie's older brother Carl said, watching the cat's open eye. "We've got to do the job ourselves." He turned to his brother and said, "Go down in our basement and get one of Dad's hammers, Ronnie."

And Ronnie, after hesitating an instant, was off, running as fast as he could the half block to their house on Tenth Street. He came back with a ballpeen hammer, so old and often employed that the pentagonal corners of the once flat steel head were almost as rounded as the smaller rear ball.

Ronnie handed the hammer to his brother and stepped back two full paces. Carl turned his hand as he grabbed the wooden handle so he held the hammer like a pendulum, with the metal head dangling down. This gesture made it clear to the other boys that he had no intention of being the executioner.

"We could draw straws," offered Pete Ferrell who, at fourteen, was the oldest and most diplomatic of the neighborhood boys.

"Not me," Ronnie said. "I'm not killing anything." And he stepped back another two paces into the street. He seemed too mortified to leave and too afraid to stay. He hunched his bare bony shoulders and shoved his hands deep into the big pockets of his cut-off blue jeans.

The cat continued to moan; rhythmically, methodically, pitifully. Michael Kardonoway turned his back on the scene and put his hands to his ears. At home he would run to his room and bury his head in the pillows of his bed when his mother was crying. After a moment he turned and took the hammer from Carl. He looked at the boys one by one. Keith Jeurgens, the best athlete in the group, met his gaze. Pete Ferrell and Gil Murdock looked down. Carl Crawford stepped back and stood next to his little brother. No one said anything.

The first blow was struck so lightly that the worn hammer head slid off the skull of the stricken cat. Michael bent down on one knee and struck again, a little harder, and the tom's whole body quivered as it received the blow. But the low moaning continued unabated. And then, with increasing velocity, Michael Kardonoway brought the ballpeen hammer down in a succession of furious blows... four, five, six. Suddenly the cat's paws stiffened and arched and began moving in death throes.

Sweat was pouring from Michael Kardonoway's face and half-naked torso as he held up the bloody instrument almost triumphantly.

The cat's head was an unrecognizable mass of blood and tissue and brain matter. The moaning had stopped.

Michael looked around at the boys whose faces all seemed to be filled with fascination and horror. He stood up and dropped the hammer at his feet. And, as he ran up the street away from his house, "Killer" Kardonoway felt no fear, no shame, no remorse. Only profound liberation.

WHAT MARY WANTED

Mary and Jim Kendall sat in sullen silence as their plane made a wide arc over the Pacific in preparation for landing at Puerto Vallarta. The argument had begun with a mild rebuke by Jim because Mary had misplaced their passports. She had defended her actions, upping the ante. Jim took offense and descended into a silent funk, closing off all further discussion.

Mary looked out the window to the horizon where the foothills of the mountains seemed to plunge into the placid bay. Instead of being pleased by the sight of what seemed to be a perfect afternoon on the first day of their vacation, Mary felt only nervous tension. The pattern of their arguments had calcified into a rigid form over twenty two years of marriage, and she knew Jim might not have a real conversation with her again for two or three days.

It was a matter of habit. Mary sometimes thought her life was totally proscribed by a complex and irrevocable set of habits. Although Jim was a successful contractor, and an adequate if not overly compassionate father to their two children, she felt the bond that held the family together was habit rather than love. Even their interactions with friends and neighbors seemed to Mary to be based more on habit than shared interests and real affection. But she didn't like to dwell on such things. It gave her a headache.

As the 727 skimmed over a cluster of mangrove trees and thudded onto the wide runway, Mary was suddenly filled with a resolve to rescue the situation; to break a habit. She leaned toward her husband and said, "Listen, Jim. Let's not start this way. This is our first vacation in three years. Puerto Vallarta seems like a beautiful place. Can't we make the most of it?" Jim, who had sat impassively as she spoke, said nothing. He reached down and struggled briefly to dislodge the carry-on shoulder bag he had stowed beneath the seat in front of him.

Mary stared at the bald spot which was spreading elliptically from the top to the back of Jim's head and tried again. This time she could feel and hear desperation creeping into her voice, "I'm sorry about the passports. You're right, it *was* stupid of me to misplace them. But I found them in plenty of time. Can't we just forget the whole thing and have some fun?"

Jim stood up in silence and without looking her way, turned his back, bending his head and shoulders uncomfortably beneath the overhead compartment. Mary watched his broad back, focusing on the strips of pale skin and white underwear exposed at his belt line where his polo shirt had pulled out of his trousers. The sight infuriated her. She wanted to lash out at this sullen brute who was about to ruin their vacation.

After clearing customs, Mary, Jim and the rest of the passengers milled about in front of the terminal waiting for the taxis and vans to arrive to take them to their hotels.

"I wish these Mexicans would get their shit together," a young man who looked to be in his mid-thirties said to Jim. "I've been to Mexico four times and there have never been any taxis at the airport when we landed."

"What do you expect from people who thought the Spaniards were gods?" Jim said. The two men chuckled wryly as Mary moved away. When the taxis did begin to arrive, Mary and Jim were separated in the scramble. Jim wedged his bulk into the front seat of a sub-compact taxi, and Mary found herself sitting next to a young man on the back seat of a battered, old VW van painted bright orange.

As the van bounced over the rough and dusty road to the Buganvilias Sheraton, Mary could feel a pleasant warmth from the young man as their shoulders and thighs jostled together in a gentle touching and parting. He had a crop of shaggy blonde hair which he kept brushing back with his left hand. He glanced at Mary and smiled. His teeth seemed to gleam in contrast to his dark tan. Mary thought he looked like a beach bum, without the regular features of that type. His nose was broken and a little too wide at the bridge, and he had a scar over his right eye.

Mary could feel a surge of sexual arousal. And as she returned the young man's smile with what she knew was much greater warmth and meaning, she felt young, young enough to be his companion.

The van turned up the curving driveway to the entrance of the hotel and jolted to an abrupt stop. The young man held Mary's elbow as she stepped down from the van. But then, as they waited for their bags to be unloaded, a yellow Toyota jeep tore up the driveway.

"Brad!" a girlish voice shouted. A young woman with long auburn hair leaped from the back seat before the jeep came to a complete stop. She was wearing cutoff jeans— short-shorts— and a white bikini top. She jumped at the young man, wrapping her legs around his waist as she kissed him full on the mouth.

"We went to the airport but we missed you, man", the driver of the jeep said. He was about the same age as Brad. Sitting shotgun was a blonde examining her nails. "Get your ass in gear," the driver continued. "We're outta here this afternoon to some island. You won't believe this sailboat, bro. It's at least thirty feet long." And in a minute Brad had loaded his canvas bags, sprung into the jeep, and was gone.

Mary felt as though she had been struck in the stomach. Her sense of loss was so intense, and so out of proportion to what had actually happened she thought for a moment that she might be losing her mind. She steadied herself against a concrete pillar and shaded her eyes as she peered into the lobby. She finally made out the red and white striped polo shirt; her husband checking in at the front counter.

Mary gathered herself and went to stand beside him. They followed the bellman to their fourth floor room in silence. Still feeling queasy, emotionally drained, Mary went straight to the bathroom, locked the door and ran the water. She soaked a towel in the wash basin while she took off her white linen traveling suit and underwear. Sitting naked on the edge of the bathtub, feeling flushed and unsteady, she patted her face, her underarms, her thighs with the wet towel. After a few minutes she lay down on the cool Spanish tile floor and pressed the towel to her eyes.

Mary didn't know how long she had been in the bathroom, but when she wrapped herself in a bath towel and opened the door, Jim had already unpacked and left the room. A wave of relief ran through

Mary. She felt sufficiently composed to unpack and put on her bathing suit. She stood in front of the full length mirror attached to the closet door and examined her image, first from the side, then, looking over her shoulder, from the rear. Her red and black one piece suit was cut low enough to reveal the tops of her breasts. The French cut legs accentuated her best feature, her long sinewy limbs. But Mary could not ignore the fact that at forty-five gravity was taking its toll. She pulled at the loose skin at the back of her thighs in disgust.

The room was in a corner of the hotel. And, just as the brochure had described it, there was a vista down the rim of the Bay of Banderas, including the Sierra Madre Mountains, as well as a view straight out to sea. Mary walked out onto the balcony, closed her eyes, and turned her face up to the tropical, mid-afternoon sun. The beach was crowded with sun worshipers seemingly oblivious to the more active fun-seekers who threw themselves at the ceaselessly pounding waves of the Pacific.

Turning her attention to the hotel pool, Mary noticed that almost every deck chair was occupied. It took her a few moments to find Jim. He was wearing his lime green boxer-style trunks, but he had on a tee shirt and towels covered his lower legs and feet. Only his face was exposed to the sun, and it was covered with white sun block. Mary decided to go to the beach.

The fine beige sand was deep and hot enough to sting the tops of her feet as Mary trudged in her flip flops toward a relatively open spot on the beach. A steady southern breeze blew up the coast, fluttering her beach towel so that she had to struggle to get it to lie flat on the sand. She anchored one corner with her flip flops, another with her paperback mystery novel, and the final two with little piles of sand. Feeling the whole ordeal was far more work than she had deserved, Mary finally lay back heavily on the towel with a sigh of relief.

Slowly, by degrees, the warmth of the sun, the soothing sound of the insistent surf, the curiously pleasant smell of a mixture of suntan lotions and the sea began to ease Mary into a state of relaxation. Five hours ago, when her plane had lifted off from the runway at Lambert Field in St. Louis, it was four degrees above zero she thought. And now, paradise. She closed her eyes as tightly as she could against the brilliant sun until she had the pleasant sensation of watching a kaleidoscopic display on the inside of her eyelids— black to purple to red to orange with flashes of light not unlike small explosions when she fluttered her lids. It was a game she had loved to play in the sun since she was a child. Within minutes she was drifting in and out of a delicious sleep.

She felt the object coming toward her before it landed with a soft thud inches from her shoulder. She woke with a start and turned her head toward the black and white ball which had been half swallowed by the deep, soft sand. And then the sun was being blocked by a solid figure.

"I'm sorry," the figure was saying. "It's stupid of us to be playing soccer near so many people." And now Mary's eyes came into focus, and she could see the wide apologetic smile on the dark face, the young body in a pair of royal blue bikini trunks. "It didn't hit you, did it?"

"No, no, not even close," Mary lied. "Besides that's what beaches are for, aren't they? Playing?" She smiled at the pleasant-looking young man as he bent to retrieve the ball. He hesitated for a moment and she found herself saying, "In fact that's the Spanish word for beach, isn't it? *Playa?*" She felt a sudden flush of warmth in her face and neck and didn't know if it was the beginning of a sunburn or a reaction to her foolish garrulousness.

"That's right. That's very good. English is my second language and I never made that connection." He smiled again, this time with the full force of an obviously practiced charm. "Well," he said as he got to his feet and stepped back, "I'm sorry anyway for disturbing you."

"You speak English very well," Mary said quickly, halting his retreat.

"Hey Juan, throw us the ball man if you're gonna talk to the beach bunnies," one of a group of young Mexican men shouted from the water's edge. Juan turned, took one step and kicked the ball expertly in a high arc twenty or thirty yards past the shoreline into the sea.

"It looks like I owe you another apology," Juan said, turning back toward Mary and again blocking the sun. She was sitting up now, leaning on her elbows, fully awake and alert. She wondered if her face still had that blurred look of sleep.

"Your friends are pretty far away. It's been a long time since I could have even thought of myself as a beach bunny," Mary laughed, a little too loudly she thought afterwards. But she didn't want Juan to leave so she plunged ahead. "Where did you learn to speak English so well?" she asked.

"My family moved to L.A. when I was ten. I graduated from U.C.L.A. two years ago, and now I vacation in Mexico just like a lot of other Californians," Juan said as he sat down in the sand beside Mary. She followed his eyes to her diamond engagement ring and wedding band. "Are you from California, Mrs...?"

"Mary," she said, consciously not offering a last name. "I'm from St. Louis.".

"I'm Juan Mendoza," he said as he put out his left hand. Mary looked into his dark eyes as his warm hand gently closed around hers. "So, you and your husband are vacationing in Puerto Vallarta?"

"Actually my husband is in Mexico City on business for a few days, and then he's flying over to join me here." Mary looked down quickly after uttering this blatant lie and pretended to brush something from her thigh. She didn't know if she was more surprised by the lie itself or by the quickness and ease of her response.

"Is this your first trip to Mexico?" Juan asked.

"Yes it is," Mary said looking up, "and although I've only been here a couple of hours, I think it's a beautiful country." Mary returned Juan's approving smile with equal warmth and hoped he didn't notice that she was furtively studying his face and body as though they were works of art. In fact, both seemed to Mary to be sculpted from fine marble, his facial features more Spanish than Indian, and his long muscles more like a swimmer's than that of most of the stocky young Mexicans she had seen on the beach. Even his thick, black hair had a sculptural quality, like a beautifully designed helmet.

"If you're free for an early dinner, I could show you the most gorgeous sunset you've ever seen in your life. There's a restaurant in the Conchas Chinas hotel called Senor Chico's with a spectacular view of the bay and the city. You can even see the ocean through the hollow crown on top of the steeple of the Church of Guadalupe." Juan's eyes seemed to dance with excitement as he gestured expansively in an apparent attempt to help her imagine the view. "The sun sets between six fifteen and six-thirty this time of year, so we would have to be there by six o'clock."

"You make it sound enticing, but I don't know. I'd have to be back at my hotel by eight to meet some friends for cocktails." Mary felt a little giddy, and was again surprised at how easily she could lie, it seemed almost pathological.

"No problem," Juan said quickly. "What time should I pick you up? Is quarter of six okay?"

Mary's mind shifted into a higher gear as she began to realize that she might actually have dinner with Juan while her husband was at the hotel. The audacity of that proposition was exhilarating, slightly frightening and, for some reason, amusing to Mary. "No," she said, smiling distractedly. "Why don't I just meet you there at six. Senor

Chico's, right?"

"Right," Juan said as he pushed himself up effortlessly. "Terrific. I've got to go finish this game of soccer with my friends. I'll see you at six. Senor Chico's in the Conchas Chinas hotel." He half-bowed and half-saluted, almost comic gestures of charming deference which were not lost on Mary, and trotted away toward the water without looking back.

Mary glanced at her Rolex; it was already past four o'clock. She lay back and tried to think rationally about what she was proposing to do: have dinner alone with a man almost half her age she had just met while on vacation with her husband in a foreign country. It was too preposterous to contemplate; but her mind was racing through a series of scenarios about how the evening could conceivably play out. It was a kind of delicious, fantastic concoction, this eclectic brew of revenge, romance and excitement simmering in her turbulent brain.

Back in her room, Mary stepped out of her bathing suit, took off her watch and jewelry, showered and put on a thick, luxurious terry cloth robe, an unexpected extra provided by the hotel. After drying her hair and putting on her make-up, she wandered out onto the balcony and searched for her husband who she presumed was still lying by the pool. He wasn't hard to find. It was almost five o'clock and the sun was low in the sky. A young couple was batting a beach ball around with their little girl in the pool. Jim Kendall was the only person still lying in a deck chair. He was apparently asleep with a towel covering his face. The towels which had covered his legs earlier in the day had slipped onto the ground. Mary could see, as far away as she was, that his thighs were the bright pink color of boiled lobster.

Instinctively, Mary felt a wave of pity for her husband. But she also felt disgust. It was the same feeling of revulsion she had experienced earlier in the day when she had seen the strip of pale skin above his belt when he had bent over in the plane. For reasons which were not entirely clear to her, these thoughts filled Mary with desolation, a terrible emptiness as she began to dress for dinner. Mary chose a sheer beige camisole and black lace panties for underwear, a black, tight skirt that was hemmed three inches above her knees, an emerald green silk blouse that buttoned down the front and a pair of comfortable black pumps. She wore her emerald and diamond necklace (a twentieth wedding anniversary present from Jim), and carried a small clamshell purse which matched her blouse. Standing before the full length mirror, she conducted a final inspection and deposited a drop of perfume behind each ear and a dab between her breasts.

On the nightstand beside their king size bed, Mary found some notepaper and a slender pen. In the crisp, efficient script of the executive secretary she had once been, Mary wrote:

>   1/18   5:35 pm
> Jim,
>   I've gone shopping in the city. Be back
> about 8 pm. I've made dinner reservations at
> the hotel restaurant for 8:30 pm.
>   Mary
> P.S. The Solarcaine is on the nightstand!

At the front desk in the lobby, Mary exchanged $100 in travelers checks into pesos, made dinner reservations for 8:30 at the hotel's best restaurant, Alejandro's, and sat down in a surprisingly comfortable bamboo chair. Just when she had decided to end the foolishness she had been contemplating and return to her room, Mary caught sight of Jim through the giant glass doors which led to the pool area. He seemed to be arguing vehemently with the clerk at the pool shack where towels were dispensed to the sunbathers. She pushed herself up and walked quickly to the hotel entrance. In the taxi, heading up the hillside to the Conchas Chinas hotel, Mary had the profound feeling that she was fleeing for her life.

II

Juan Mendoza was waiting for Mary at the entrance to the hotel lobby. He was wearing a long sleeve royal blue shirt (his favorite color, she thought) which shimmered slightly in the late afternoon light, black pleated trousers, and black shoes with very high heels and pointed toes. Mary thought Juan had to be the only person she had ever known who looked significantly better in swimming trunks than in street clothes.

The maitre de, who like Juan looked European, seated them at a table on a covered balcony overlooking the city and the bay. The view was indeed breathtaking, even more spectacular than she had imagined from Juan's animated description. The brown, orange and gray tile roofs cascaded down the hillside to the main town square, the *zocolo*, and the arresting presence of the Church of Guadalupe. An eight sided clock tower above the steeple provided a pedestal for an intricately designed hollow metal crown through which Mary could see the sparkling sea, just as Juan had said.

The sun, a huge orange disc balanced just above the horizon, completed the postcard setting, although Mary thought there was nothing banal about the scene. It was so immediate, so vibrant and it made her feel so glad to be alive that she decided to never try to describe it to anyone.

"You know Mary, no matter how often I climb the hills around this city, I never look at a sunset complacently. Each sunset is a gift, and this one is made sweeter by your company." Juan raised his glass of Mexican wine and Mary raised hers. He's too beautiful and he's too full of shit for me to feel so happy, she thought.

"What was your major at U.C.L.A.," Mary asked in an attempt to deflect the mesmerizing power the setting sun and Juan's charm were having on her emotions.

"I majored in film," Juan replied without hesitation. "I work for Paramount Studios now. I was the `Best Boy' on my first location," he said with a laugh. "That's a film makers term for `go- fer'; but it's a start. It gives me a chance to learn the craft."

"It sounds exciting to me," Mary said with genuine interest. "What was the name of the picture?"

"It was a real dog aimed at the teen market called *My Sister's Boyfriend*. But some day I hope to work on interesting films like John Huston's *Night of the Iguana* which was shot just outside of Puerto Vallarta."

"Really," Mary said, remembering uncomfortably that she had seen that movie during its first run in St. Louis in the 1960s.

"If you're free tomorrow I could take you to the exact location. Mismaloya. It's about six or seven miles south, right on the beach. Huston fell in love with Mexico while he was making that film and the house he built is still there," Juan said earnestly, as though he were answering a question in class.

Mary noticed that the restaurant staff was treating them politely, but with a kind of aloofness which made her aware of how they must appear; the middle-aged American lady with her Mexican gigolo. And that description was right on target, she thought. It was a sobering thought. She could feel the exhilarating joy of the evening slipping away. "I think I have to go on a fishing expedition tomorrow," she said distractedly.

The waiter brought Mary the check. Juan did not protest, and now that she was willing to accept the obvious truth of the situation (could she really have been that self-deceiving?), she paid the bill with her American Express card.

As they reached the stairs at the front entrance to the hotel, Juan grabbed Mary's elbow and gently turned her to face him. "It's only ten after seven," he said. "At the top of this hill there is a clearing with an even more spectacular view than from the restaurant. Now that it's dark, you can see the lights of the city in every direction from there."

"I don't think so..." Mary began.

"My motor scooter will climb the hill in five minutes," Juan said. "We'll be back here by seven-thirty."

Mary suddenly felt very tired. Her mind reeled through a list of potential terrors. He could beat me. He could rob me. He could rape me. He could kill me. I'd be defenseless. She felt herself sway toward Juan and he caught her other elbow as she fell against him. And now she knew what she really felt: sexual arousal.

"Are you okay?" Juan asked with what seemed like genuine concern.

"Let's go," Mary said. And Juan smiled with what she thought was the delight of a child rather than the triumph of a conqueror.

The motor scooter was designed for two people, but Mary had to raise her tight skirt to the top of her thighs to straddle the seat. She wrapped her arms around Juan's hard body and pressed her face between his shoulders as they tore up the winding lane to the top of the hill. She felt exposed but not ashamed.

They had to climb the last thirty yards on foot up a narrow path to the summit and the clearing. The night air felt clean and surprisingly cool. Mary knew that even the most spectacular scenery could become tiresome after a while. But the mood was right and her satisfaction was almost complete.

"Before I was born, Puerto Vallarta was just a little fishing village," Juan said. "Now, mainly because of the tourists, over 200,000 people live here." A jumbo jet passed low in the sky over their heads as if to confirm his words.

Mary again thought Juan sounded like a student answering a question in class. His seeming innocence made her feel maternal (the thought that she was old enough to be his mother had already crossed her mind) and, at the same time, made her want him all the more. She lifted her face to him and he kissed her gently on the mouth. And then she was in his arms and he was raining kisses all over her face and neck. He slid his hands down her back and lifted her skirt. With a hand on each buttock he pulled her up and into his body as he probed her open and willing mouth with his tongue. Mary felt the full flush of sexual arousal as Juan pressed her against his hard member.

"No," Mary said as she pushed him away firmly. "I can't do this." She took a deep breath as she pulled her skirt down and then brushed her hair back with both hands. "I'm very attracted to you, Juan, but I can't do this." She looked into his eyes trying to gauge his reaction, but she could read nothing beyond a mild surprise. And then Juan's face became a mask of seeming indifference.

"Whatever," he said with a shrug as he turned to walk toward his scooter.

Mary put her hands on the back of the seat and tried not to touch Juan as he expertly guided the motor scooter through the steep turns on the way back to the Conchis Chinas hotel. She quickly lifted herself off the scooter at the entrance to the hotel and, without saying a word, walked swiftly to a taxi that was waiting nearby. As the taxi turned toward the hotel exit, Juan sped by and raised his hand in a salute as he had done earlier that day at the beach. He was smiling, what Mary thought was a sardonic smile.

Fuck you she thought, as tears welled into her eyes. You could have had me, you spic bastard.

THE LESSON

My first day alone in the field as a salesman of microfilm products for the Microfax Corporation was not going well. It was 1978 and microfilm for the office was a dying industry on the verge of becoming a victim of the desktop computer revolution. But I didn't know that. All I knew was that I was married, I had an eigtheen-month old daughter, and that I was behind in my apartment rent, my stereo payment, and my furniture loan.

The Company's advertising agency had mounted a massive and expensive direct mail campaign that promised a free gift to anyone who would listen to a sales pitch in person. That gift was a book called *Golf My Way* by Jack Nicklaus. The mailers were sent to presidents of mid-size companies and to owners of smaller businesses. The campaign had generated hundreds of leads, most of which the sales force soon found out were of dubious quality.

I hadn't been able to get past the secretary on my first call at Queen City Brewery, even though I had an appointment. Julie Evans was a spectacular blonde who, after showing a momentary flirtatious interest in the way I looked, soon seemed to size me up as a small fish. Giving me a cold eye, she said her boss, Paul Koestler, had been unexpectedly called into an important meeting and had given instructions for me to leave the Jack Nicklaus book with her. She said I could call the following week to set up another appointment. Fat chance.

I reluctantly gave her the book and, as I was leaving, I glanced through the half-open door to Koestler's office. He was sitting back in his executive chair with his feet propped on his desk, reading the sports section of *The Cincinnati Enquirer* and sipping a cup of coffee.

My second call had been at Kruptmeyer Bakery on Vine Street not far from downtown. I arrived about five minutes early and the comptroller, Morris Weinman, had kept me waiting at least thirty minutes. When I finally did get in to see him, Weinman accepted his Jack Nicklaus book in silence and fixed me with a dour expression. He had begun to move his head from side to side during the third sentence of my presentation.

"How much is this going to cost, Mr. Menendez?", Weinman interrupted as he pushed out his lower lip and continued to shake his head "no." He began reading the blurb on the back of the Nicklaus book.

"Well, that depends," I had said, brightening, remembering what Steve Farris, my sales trainer, had told me about buying signals. "A basic Microfax system could be as little as $5,000 for what I think you'll probably need."

"And how do you know what we'll probably need, Mr. Menendez?", Weinman had said as he began shuffling through some papers on his desk.

"That's what I'm here to find out," I said. "I'm here to find out what you need and how the Microfax Corporation can fulfill those needs." That line was almost a verbatim quote from the Microfax sales training manual. It had a hollow ring when I first read it and it sounded even worse when I found it coming out of my mouth.

"Yes, well, why don't you leave your card with my secretary, Mr. Menendez, and we'll keep you in mind when our needs become more apparent." Weinman had begun writing and he didn't look up as I left his office. I sat in my company car, a lime green Chevy Caprice with so few frills it could have easily been mistaken for a plain wrapper highway patrol car, and wondered what I was going to do with the two and a half hours until my next appointment at one-thirty. I really didn't blame Weinman for giving me such short shrift. Although at twenty-five I had just graduated from Xavier University with a marketing degree (working my way through college by bartending at Charlie Brown's), my Irish mother and Mexican father had produced a child who, as my wife often playfully reminded me, grew into manhood with cheeks and brow as clean and smooth as his daughter's ass. Not exactly a vision of savvy competence to inspire trust in the hearts and minds of fifty year-old executives.

I drove down Vine Street into the heart of Cincinnati and parked near Fountain Square. I killed forty-five minutes playing pin-ball machines in a pool hall just off the Square. Then I flipped a coin to decide if I would eat lunch at La Rosa's Pizza or Skyline Chili. Skyline won and I ordered a bowl of three-way chili with beans, spaghetti and cheese. I think they added some onions to my order, because that chili churned my stomach like a cheap blender. I strolled around the square belching chili three ways and cursing my stupidity.

The early afternoon October sun broke through the morning cloud cover. The mostly female office workers and sales clerks lunching on the Square took off their fall jackets and sweaters and stretched their young bodies toward the warmth of the sun. The thought crossed my mind that I could've probably talked one of those lovelies into taking the afternoon off to goof around with me up on Mt. Adams or in Eden Park. It seemed a terrific alternative to having my ego battered by balding and paunchy old men the rest of the day.

The International Brotherhood of Electrical Workers offices were housed in a nondescript limestone building on Colerain Avenue. The only ornamentation was two fluted Greek columns flanking the entrance and a bronze relief sculpture above the doorway of two muscular arms with their oversized hands grasping each other at the wrists.

I put my new vinyl briefcase between my feet and checked out my reflection in the glass door. I straightened the half-Windsor knot in my rep tie and shot my cuffs. Then I lowered my head as I picked up my briefcase and stepped into what I thought of as the fray. My appointment was with Herman Schuler, Executive Director of the Cincinnati chapter of the Electrical Workers Union. I found the glass door bearing his name and title and walked in smiling. My smile was met by an even broader one on the face of Schuler's secretary and assistant whose nameplate on her desk said: Mrs. Carolyn Deckard. She was a bright and pleasant woman whom I guessed to be in her late forties or early fifties. Carolyn Deckard stood up and walked around her green metal desk to greet me. Although she was more than a little overweight, she moved with the grace and energy of a former dancer. I liked her immediately.

"I'll bet you're Ray Menendez of the Microfax Corporation," she said happily. "I'm Carolyn Deckard and, boy, am I glad to see you."

She shook my hand firmly and took off her tortoise shell glasses which were attached to a corded neck strap. "Put down your briefcase and follow me."

I put my briefcase on a straight back wooden chair beside her desk and obediently followed her across the room. There were three other women working in the large unpartitioned office, all about the same age or older than Carolyn Deckard. She introduced me to each of them as we passed their desks. They didn't seem to share Mrs. Deckard's enthusiasm for my arrival.

At the opposite end of the room from her desk and Schuler's office Carolyn Deckard stopped before a huge metal vault door that was slightly ajar. I helped her push it open. Inside was a microfilm equipment salesman's dream come true— a cavernous vault with row after row of file cabinets and boxes and horizontal card files literally overflowing with documents of every conceivable shape, size and color.

"We've got membership cards and other records in here dating from 1923, but I'll be damned if I know where they are," Mrs. Deckard said to me as she walked down the rows of file cabinets, randomly opening drawers and fanning through the documents in selected folders. She stopped abruptly and put on her glasses. She lowered them slightly and peered over the top edges at me and said coyly, "Do you think you can help us out here, Ray?" And then she laughed and took my arm and walked me back to her desk.

I explained what I thought it would take to reduce the nightmare of documentation contained in that vault into cartridges of 16mm microfilm that would fit on the top of her desk. I showed her the odometer system that would allow her and her colleagues to retrieve any document in less than a minute. I discussed the Microfax reader-printer that would enable them to make a plain paper copy of any page in two seconds. I went over the two cameras which would be required; an overhead camera for the ledger books, other bound records and oversized documents and an automatic-feeding rotary camera for loose sheets of any length up to fourteen inches wide.

Carolyn Deckard's attention never wandered. She followed my presentation, making careful notes and asking pertinent and timely questions about anything she didn't fully understand. When she seemed satisfied, I took out an order form from the back of my presentation binder and we wrote up the order together. Two cameras, two reader-printers and two readers. Fifty rolls of microfilm to start and cabinets for all of the equipment and software. The total order amounted to $22,546.00, not including tax and shipping charges. Carolyn Deckard didn't flinch at the amount. She had already checked out the competition and immediately knew that our prices were lower in most cases. Oh sweet joyful day. I quickly calculated my 15% commission to be about $3,400. Thirty-four hundred dollars my first day on the job. I would be a hero at the home office of the Microfax Corporation. More importantly, I could catch up on my back rent and stereo payment, and pay off my furniture loan.

"Well, all that's left to do now is to get Herman's approval." Carolyn Deckard's words jolted me out of my reverie. She must have seen the cloud pass over my face because she reached out her hand and patted me maternally on my arm and said, "Now don't worry. Herman Schuler is a very reasonable man. I'll go in and soften him up and then you come in and finish him off." She smiled at me conspiratorially and walked into Schuler's office without knocking.

Although Carolyn Deckard was only in Herman Schuler's office for a few minutes, it seemed like an eternity. At last she opened the door and beckoned me to come in. I tried to read the smile on her face, but all my powers of perception seemed to have abandoned me. All I could think of was $3,400.

Mrs. Deckard introduced me to Herman Schuler and slipped out of the office, closing the door as she left. The door thudded and clicked shut with an ominous finality.

"Sit.", Herman Schuler said, motioning me to a light green metal chair with a dark green padded seat which stood beside his huge mahogany desk. Herman Schuler was a mountain of flesh. He had no neck; only a monumental bald head that cascaded into and over the collar of his faded white shirt. Big stains of perspiration spread from his underarms like Rorschach ink blots. He was wearing a wide red and gold floral tie, one that he could have bought in the 1940s. The knot was the size of a baseball and was shoved up, into and under the folds of his many chins, making him look terrifically uncomfortable.

"Raymond Mendez," he said distractedly as he rubbed his bulbous nose.

"Menendez," I quickly corrected him out of habit, without thinking.

"That's what I said, Mendez. That a Mexican name?" His lips were so big I could see no teeth. In fact, all of his features were large so his lips looked reasonably in proportion to his huge head.

"My father was Mexican," I said, trying not to sound defensive, "and my mother was Irish."

"Fellow by the name of Manny Consuelo taught me everything I know about wiring a building. He ran the crew that rewired the old Cincinnati Milling Machine building up on Price Hill. The sonofabitch knew his stuff. Manny's original union membership card is somewhere in that fucking vault." He waved one of his huge hands, with deep dimples where knuckles should have been, toward the outer room and the now infamous vault where documents went to die. Thirty-four hundred dollars. "So what have you got?" he said abruptly.

"Well, I've got a system that will help you find Manny Consuelo's membership card and any other record in that vault in a matter of seconds," I said. I felt confident now, but Schuler just looked at me blankly.

"Hand me a cigar from that humidor on my desk and help yourself to one," he said.

"Thank you, but I don't smoke." I handed him a huge cigar with a plainly marked Havana wrapper, wondering if I had offended him by refusing his offer. He pulled a gold lighter from his pocket with some difficulty, bit the end off his cigar and spat the small wad of tobacco expertly into a wastebasket next to his chair. He lit the cigar carefully and luxuriantly as only a true cigar connoisseur knows how to do, or cares to do.

"Churchills. Fucking Castro commies make great cigars. What can I say?" His face was obscured for several seconds by thick white smoke as he exhaled and suppressed a cough. When the smoke cleared, his face was still a mask of seeming uninterest.

We looked at each other for several seconds. Long enough for me to feel the uncomfortable silence. Not knowing what else to do, I finally said, "Let me show you the system, Mr. Schuler," as I bent over to take my presentation binder out of my briefcase. I fingered Schuler's Jack Nicklaus book for a second, but had to smile at the thought of this elephant of a man swinging at a little golf ball. "Do you mind if I pull my chair around and go through this with you?"

He shrugged with the corners of his enormous mouth and a slight tremor of his shoulders. I began going through the presentation as I had done with Mrs. Deckard, but after the first few sentences I could see Herman Schuler's huge frog-lidded eyes glaze over in boredom and what I thought was disbelief. A sinking feeling surged through me as I plunged on, vowing not to look at that huge face again. As I skimmed through the presentation, skipping sections, mechanically and unenthusiastically muttering the words, I knew I had blown the sale. In a deep funk, I swore I would never, never ever begin spending my commission until after the order was signed and delivered.

Suddenly I felt a hand on my shoulder, but it was so out-sized and heavy I thought this is what a grizzly bear's paw must feel like.

"Ray, do me a favor, will you?" Schuler interrupted.

"What's that?" I asked without looking up from my binder, true to my vow not to look at him again.

"Open that bottom desk drawer there by your feet."

I opened it.

"What do you see there, Ray?"

"It looks like a bottle of whiskey," I said, smiling despite my gloom.

"Maker's Mark," Schuler said. "Twelve years old. What's behind that bottle, Ray?"

"Why, it looks like a couple of double shot glasses, Mr. Schuler," I said, playing along with his game. What else could I do?

"Correct-a-mundo Raymundo," Schuler said jovially. "Why don't you remove that precious decanter and decant us a nip? You do drink, don't you, Ray?" He asked this last question seriously and without apparent malice.

"Yes sir, Mr. Schuler, I do have a drink now and then," I answered evenly. "But to tell the truth, my drink of choice is not bourbon and I rarely drink before five o'clock." I figured since the sale was blown I had nothing to lose by being blunt.

"That's fair enough. But before you make that decision final, can I ask you a question or two?" Schuler said. I broke my vow and looked at his face. He was smiling. He did his smiling mostly with his big froggy eyes. Who would have thought they could look so soft and watery and mischievous?

"Will that `system', as you call it, that you showed Carolyn make little ones out of big ones?" he began. I nodded. "And will Carolyn and Sylvia and Bernice and Rhonda be able to find what they want? Or what *I* want?" I nodded again. "And will you and your company stand behind that equipment? Remember now, I'm an electrician by trade. I know electro-mechanical devices break down." I nodded without hesitating. "Then son, why don't you shut the fuck up and sell it to me?"

Herman Schuler signed the order form just as Carolyn Deckard and I had written it. I drank a double shot of Maker's Mark with him to celebrate the sale, and when Schuler renewed his offer to share a cigar with him, I accepted without hesitation. As I was about to leave Schuler put up a finger to stop me.

"Where's my Jack Nicklaus book, Ray?"

"Gee, I'm sorry, Mr. Schuler," I said, feeling a flush come to my face. "I guess in the excitement of my first sale I forgot all about it." I snapped open my briefcase and fumbled for the book, feeling stupid and ashamed for lying.

Schuler must have noticed my discomfort because his eyes softened again and he said, "That's okay, Ray. You wouldn't think a fat fuck like me could play golf. Do you play?"

"About twice a year," I said, relieved to be able to tell a humble truth. "I bought a set of used clubs at a garage sale a couple of years ago. I'm a real hacker. I've never broken 120."

"Don't feel bad. Golf's a hard game," Schuler said as he began to read the copy on the back cover of the Jack Nicklaus book. *Golf My Way*, he said absently. "Shit, nobody can play golf his way. I played him in the semifinals of the 1956 Ohio Open. I was thirty-five and Nicklaus was only sixteen years old. He kicked my ass all over the course." Then Schuler began to chuckle. "That bastard was fatter than I was back then. Fat Jack. That was his first big tournament win. In 1962, his first full year as a pro, he didn't play in the Ohio Open and I won it."

He was deep in his memories now, not really talking to me. "Herman the German. That was my nickname. Got it because my dad was my caddy and he had a thick German accent." He fell silent, remembering, and I felt like an intruder.

"So you still play," I said, trying hard to keep any hint of incredulity out of my voice.

"I'm a nine at River Glen," he said matter-of-factly. "That's what's great about golf, Ray. It's just like life. You can still play and learn something about the game even when you're 59 and weigh 300 pounds." He chuckled again and pushed himself up with considerable effort. Schuler put his big beefy arm around my shoulders as he walked me to the door. And I remembered what Steve Farris had told me during one of our sales training sessions. He said that if you could get a guy to let you put your hands on him, then you had him. You were probably going to make the sale.

What if you let *him* put his hands on you, I thought as I walked to my car. I patted the sales contract which I had carefully folded and placed in the inside pocket of my suit coat. And then, for a minute, as I took a deep drag on the fat Havana cigar Schuler had given me, I considered changing my name to Mendez.

WEIGHTS AND MEASURES

In 1952, when he was sixty-eight years old, my grandfather, Demitrius Pendrakis, became a dangerously unpredictable man. After watching fifteen minutes of the Army/McCarthy hearings on our new Philco TV, my grandfather became a card-carrying member of the Communist Party. He taped the card to the back of the framed color photo of Franklin Roosevelt which had hung in our upstairs hallway for as long as I could remember. "I'm sorry, Mr. President," my grandfather said to Roosevelt's image. "But if you ask me, Joe McCarthy looks like a fascist pervert who makes nasty with little boys."

That same year, my grandfather started closing his diner on Tuesdays instead of Sundays. Pete's Diner. "I like the name Pete," he explained to those who asked. When customers complained about the new day of closing he said, "Who needs meatloaf and mashed potatoes on Tuesday?" He did it so he could do the family shopping. For reasons still not clear to me, my grandfather never brought food home from his diner. And our family seldom ate there. That summer, right after my eleventh birthday, I started helping him with the shopping at my mother's request. My two older brothers had summer jobs. I soon found that hardly anyone else shopped on Tuesday morning. This suited my grandfather fine because it allowed him to engage the various merchants in protracted, and often heated arguments (he called them "conversations") about politics or business or religion.

My grandfather once told Sol Wiseman, our butcher, who had a reputation for putting his thumb on the scale, that he, my grandfather, would be an atheist if it weren't for the Byzantine icons in the St. Nicholas Greek Orthodox Church ("They make me feel peaceful," he said), and the rituals of the mass. "Stand up, sit down, get on your knees, answer the priest, make the cross, amen. Forget the foolish stories that fill up the Bible. I like the slow and steady predictability of the holy liturgy compared to the craziness of a lunch rush at my diner."

"It seems to me that you *are* an atheist," Wiseman said. "All you really believe in is pretty pictures and empty rituals."

"Not so," my grandfather replied evenly. "God is most alive for me when He is guiding the hand of an artist; when He is creating order out of chaos."

"Order out of chaos? Pshaw," Wiseman muttered in disgust. "That old, mawkish cliché. You'll have to come up with something better than that sentimental goo."

"I can't help it if the truth, *my* truth, sounds like mawkish sentimentality to a great scholar like you, Rabbi Wiseman," my grandfather said, rolling the "r" in rabbi in an exaggerated way. "Truth is truth." The fact is Wiseman was as superstitious as my grandfather. Wiseman believed that if the first customer of the day didn't make a substantial purchase it would be a bad day. Sometimes, when they were feuding, my grandfather would camp out on Wiseman's doorstep first thing in the morning to be the first customer. Then, of course, he wouldn't make a purchase just to get Wiseman's goat. It was a ritual.

Our weekly shopping expeditions were ritualized, too. Every Tuesday we took the 7:30 a.m. streetcar to the open air Soulard market to shop for fruits and vegetables. From there we would walk to Kaesine's fish house, a block from the river, to buy jack salmon. An hour and a half later, back in our own neighborhood, we went to Hauptmann's bakery. At nine fifteen, we stopped at home to drop off our purchases and to eat the breakfast my mother had waiting: Turkish coffee and a fresh sweet roll from Hauptmann's for my grandfather; scrambled eggs, toast and orange juice for me.

After breakfast, we went to Thornton's grocery to buy canned goods, eggs and condiments; and then, at about 10:15, we always made our final stop of the morning at Sol Wiseman's butcher shop. The combative Wiseman, who was also approaching seventy, was my grandfather's favorite antagonist.

The Tuesday Wiseman died, my grandfather had pinned an enormous *I LIKE IKE* button on his lapel before we entered the shop at about 10:30. He did it because he knew Wiseman was an ardent Stevenson supporter.

"You're late, you miserable Greek hypocrite," Wiseman shouted from behind the display case when he saw the button. Wiseman was waiting on Mrs. Zavorkian, whose husband had recently been killed in the Korean war. She had three young children whom she struggled to support by working the second shift at a hat factory. My grandfather said nothing as he pretended to examine the various cuts of meat in the display case. I could see him watching out of the corner of his eye as Wiseman weighed Mrs. Zavorkian's purchases.

When the transaction was completed and Mrs. Zavorkian, dressed in black from her scarf to her shoes, left the shop, my grandfather leaned against the counter near the cash register and said, "Who you calling a hypocrite? You think I'm blind? Instead of the thumb on the scale, which I guess you reserve for me, you're now selling levitating lunch meat, hovering hamburger, lighter-than-air pork chops?"

"What are you talking about, Mr. I like Ike?"

"Don't try and change the subject. I'm wise to you Mr. Wise-man. You've gone soft. Your weights and measures don't measure up." My grandfather was smiling now, grinning from ear to ear. "It's guys like you who murder stereotypes. The Jewish merchant with a heart of gold."

"The world is a sad place for people like Edith Zavorkian," Wiseman said as he took off his glasses and rubbed his eyes hard with his fists. "The only book that ever meant anything to me is the Book of Job."

"I love you three slices of pickle loaf. I love you four ounces of hamburger. I love you two pork chops," my grandfather intoned, not unlike a Gregorian chanter. Not mocking. "I get the picture." He paused for only a second and said in a belligerent voice, "So, you want to know why I like Ike, huh Wiseman?"

"Now who's changing the subject, Mr. Demitrius Pendrakis."

My grandfather plunged ahead, "I like Ike because although he was a great soldier, he was an even greater politician. Only a great politician could have held the allies and their pig-headed generals together to win the Second World War."

"All the way with Adlai!" Wiseman shouted. "I'd rather have a man with a hole in his shoe than a general with a hole in his head." Years later I learned he was referring to a famous photo of Stevenson with his legs crossed revealing a hole which had been worn in the sole of his shoe.

    They continued ranting at one another, like mortal enemies, for at least fifteen minutes before we left the shop. When we returned to our house, my grandfather went upstairs to take a nap. I tucked my Marty Marion baseball glove under my arm and took off to join the sandlot games that went on all day at Tower Grove park. My route took me right by Wiseman's butcher shop.

    I was eating a bag of sunflower seeds, the last in my life, when I rounded the corner and saw the ambulance workers carrying Sol Wiseman's body on a stretcher. Later I found out a vessel had burst in his temple while he was carrying a slab of beef out of the freezer. He died almost instantly.

    My mother waited until that evening to tell my grandfather. He wouldn't let us turn on the TV or radio until after the funeral. My mother said the day Wiseman was buried was the first time she had seen my grandfather cry since he learned my father had been killed in the battle for Iwo Jima.

    Mrs. Wiseman sold the butcher shop. The new owners remodeled the interior and replaced most of the equipment. My grandfather paid them five dollars for Wiseman's old scale.

THE VOICE OF THE TITANS

Howard Cantrell, the Voice of the Toledo Titans, was through. The telegram, bearing the bad news, was still in the inside pocket of his impeccably tailored navy blue blazer. He drove toward J. Edgar Hoover Memorial Stadium in the splendid early afternoon sunlight, knowing he would announce only one more Titan home game: his last. After over thirty years of loyal service, he didn't even rate a phone call. But from his contract negotiations with team owner Adolph Seinsheimer III, Cantrell knew there was a certain appropriateness to the impersonal and anachronistic use of Western Union to deliver the ultra-conservative beer baron's final word on any important matter.

Cantrell had been relaxing in his recently installed jacuzzi with his nubile young secretary Lisa Fox when the message was delivered to his condominium. Still wet and wrapped in his Italian silk robe, Cantrell had read the telegram over and over as he stood before the wall of windows in his bedroom. He glanced over at Lisa, but she was oblivious to his anguish. Her head was thrown back, eyes closed in rapture as she pleasured herself by sitting on one of the jets which churned the 104 degree water in the tiled hot tub. Lisa was twenty-seven, exactly half Cantrell's age. Although she had long, sinewy limbs, slim hips and a flat stomach, she was as well-endowed as any centerfold model. Cantrell thought Lisa's body was exactly what The First Mover had in mind when he had created woman. Her shoulder-length hair was the rich color of Jonathan apples and her sleepy eyes were a liquid dark brown— another combination Cantrell found irresistible.

   His condo was situated on a promontory point which commanded an expansive view of thick, verdant woods, and, in the distance, the murky waters of Lake Erie. The subdued late afternoon sun had lingered quietly on the horizon. The serenity of this view belied the roiling in Cantrell's stomach. He walked aimlessly from room to room. After his most recent and particularly acrimonious divorce, Cantrell had wanted to expunge every vestige of his ex-wife's presence in his home. Out went the fussiness of her Queen Anne furniture, her paintings by Turner and Constable copyists, her plush pastel carpeting and heavy drapes. In came sleek Spanish leather couches and teak parsons tables, oriental rugs, hardwood floors and original prints by Picasso and Braque. And, of course, he had installed that new state of the art wave-producing jacuzzzi in his bedroom. A sauna and steamroom on the broad deck overlooking the woods completed his concept of the ultimate bachelor pad.

   Cantrell had been introduced to what he considered the finer things in life as a scholarship undergraduate at Columbia University in New York City. He had majored in journalism and minored in statistics. But his true and abiding love was baseball. He had begun collecting baseball cards at the age of six when he lived on a farm near Lincoln, Nebraska. And, even though he wasn't talented enough to make his high school team, as a teenager he had immersed himself in the seemingly endless array of statistics which could be compiled on all the aspects of the game.

   In fact, his final paper at Columbia had been a finely reasoned debate on whether Joe DiMaggio's fifty-six game hitting streak in 1941 or Babe Ruth's lifetime slugging percentage of .690 was, statistically speaking, the greatest achievement in sport.

   One whole room of his condo was devoted to his collection of baseball statistics and memorabilia amassed over almost fifty years, including the baseball cards he had collected as a boy. All of it was meticulously catalogued and indexed for instant retrieval. But it was both Cantrell's encyclopedic baseball knowledge and his distinctive voice which had landed him his first job in radio. As a cub sports reporter for *The New York Mirror*, his questions were so intelligent, asked in such a resonant and well-modulated tone, that even the most aggressive and jaded veteran reporters would defer to him in a crowded locker room.

After only one year of announcing for the Titan farm team in Birmingham, Adolph Seinsheimer and his sons had brought him up to the Bigs. And now he was through. The injustice overwhelmed him. His brain buzzed and his hands trembled so badly he decided to pour himself a drink. Cantrell slumped down into his favorite reading chair, trying to relax, and ran his fingers through his gray, thinning hair. After a few minutes he pushed himself up. He felt leaden and lethargic as he walked over to the jacuzzi and explained to Lisa that he had just received some bad personal news and that he wanted to be alone. Her wide, supple mouth turned down for an instant in an exaggerated frown, but, without saying a word, she obediently lifted herself out of the tub. Cantrell felt an aching in his loins as he watched her perfectly formed buttocks sway gracefully toward his bathroom.

Lisa Fox dutifully showered and dressed in fifteen minutes and he walked her to the door in silence. Cantrell felt another twinge of regret as she bussed hls cheek in parting, leaving behind a subtle hint of perfume.

Back in his chair, a sullen Cantrell distractedly stirred his scotch and soda, which was now weakened by the melted ice. He could think of nothing but the traitorous Seinsheimers. Hadn't he been their boy? Hadn't he seen them through good times and bad with the same even, golden voice? Hadn't he been his own color man these last few games, a baseball scholar who knew more averages, facts and statistics than all the other announcers in both leagues combined? What about his funny, sometimes touching anecdotes about the baseball greats?

And who was to be his replacement? Barry Fairly. The thought sickened him. Barry Fairly, "The Screamer." To the pros, the real pros who called Cantrell the Walter Cronkite of baseball announcers, Barry Fairly was a bad joke. He always sounded as though he were announcing while hanging from a precipice, on the verge of losing both his grip and his voice. He was very fond of expletives like "Holy Cow!" and , "It might be, it could be, by golly, it *is*...," which he shouted at 100 decibels.

Cantrell knew Barry Fairly had been fired by Buffalo during the off-season for fooling around with the owner's wife. Cantrell's own contract was due to expire in October. It galled him that the Seinsheimer family was willing to let him go in mid-season to hire Barry Fairly, a Bush Leaguer. But apparently, Bush League announcing was what the old man wanted. His telegram was clear on that point: "We need someone in our broadcast booth who can convey the excitement of our explosive Titans with more zeal." Excitement and zeal— if that's what they wanted, that's what Cantrell would give them. The beginning of a plan for revenge began to germinate in his mind. A plan that would make his last game as "The Voice of the Titans" an unforgettable event.

Cantrell stayed awake all night conceiving his plan and putting the first part into operation. As he shaved and dressed at noon his mind was tired and his thin, aging body was exhausted. But he had an abundance of nervous energy from cigarettes and coffee, which he hoped would get him through the day.

He turned his S-Class Mercedes into Stadium Drive at twelve-thirty, forty-five minutes late and only fifteen minutes before the scheduled pre-game show. But that was according to plan. Cantrell didn't want to get to his broadcast booth until five minutes prior to airtime. If he succeeded, there would be no briefing for his interview with Titan field manager "Spunky" Robinson.

Former Yankee great Rusty Franklin Cantrell's color man, had been in the hospital for three days with a broken hip suffered in a boating accident. Although Cantrell had admired Franklin when he was a player and liked his straightforward honesty in the broadcast booth, he had enjoyed announcing the last few games without the ebullient and often inane interruptions from his garrulous sidekick. And now Franklin's absence fit right into Cantrell's plans, too.

After parking his Mercedes in his reserved space and entering at the press gate, Cantrell stopped to watch the people, the baseball fans, stream into the stadium. For the most part they were well-dressed and in a festive mood. Anxious little boys, with baseball gloves already on, skipping beside their fathers; young girls, who would stay after the game to get the best-looking players to autograph their scorecards; middle-aged couples, arm in arm, happy to spend a day together in the sun. They were the kind of people who could be called "typical American fans."

Cantrell heard the stadium organ playing the last few bars of "Take Me Out To The Ball Game" over the sound system as he made his way to the pay telephone booth on the ground level of the stadium.

"Good afternoon, this is Radio Station K-R-A-S, a Great Lakes Broadcasting Station." Cantrell recognized the impersonal voice of receptionist Rosemary Kellerman.

Howard Cantrell was a radio man, a radio pro who knew his voice well. He could throw his voice, as a ventriloquist does, or change it at will. For this occasion he chose a deep, guttural tone. "Listen very carefully and don't interrupt. There is a bomb planted in your building which is due to explode in exactly"— he checked his Rolex watch— "in exactly nine minutes. After that explosion others will follow at five minute intervals." And then, soberly, very seriously, he said, "This is no hoax. You now have less than nine minutes." He hung up quickly, without waiting for a reply. Cantrell was satisfied that Rosemary Kellerman, who had a tough veneer hardened by daily contact with salesmen and radio "personalities," would know the difference between a snow job and the real thing.

He walked briskly to the elevator. The thought that in a few minutes his voice would be locked into air waves leading to all the major cities in the Great Lakes broadcast area— St. Louis, Chicago, Cleveland, Detroit and even New York City— filled Cantrell with pleasurable excitement. And with the downtown station evacuated, except perhaps for a bomb squad, he could not be turned off... for at least a little while.

To assure the success of his plan he had actually planted a bomb in a remote storage room in the basement at the station. An avid reader of spy novels, Howard Cantrell had learned the mechanics of building a simple explosive device from the pages of a cheap thriller. Dressed in a Ralph Lauren pullover, a pair of lightweight gabardine slacks from his British tailor, and a pair of Gucci loafers, he had begun to comb construction sites at midnight for blasting caps and some kind of explosive. Armed with the virgin tire iron from his Mercedes, Cantrell had ripped open the lock of a walk-in construction trailer at an isolated and deserted highrise project on Canal Street just west of downtown. As he rummaged through the boxes in the trailer, a summer squall had blown in from the lake. Within minutes, the deep hole, which was to be the basement of the building, had been filled with more than an inch of water, and the barren ground around it had become a quagmire.

Cantrell had emerged from the trailer with a box of blasting caps, a small spindle of wire and two sticks of dynamite. As he stepped to the ground in the driving rain, a rat about the size of a kitten had scurried for cover beneath the trailer. The startled Cantrell had stumbled through the muck and detritus— short lengths of two by fours, empty cigarette packs, broken Coke bottles, tattered cement bags, candy wrappers— feeling like a drowned rat himself. He realized the inappropriateness of the way he had dressed, but he was in a hurry to get away from the scene of his crime now that he had what he needed. The huge wet drops had pelted him mercilessly as he ran to his car. He sped away, fish-tailing in the mud and gravel. In ten minutes the storm had ended as quickly as it had begun.

Splattered with mud, his hair matted and stuck to his forehead, his shoes encased in boots of concrete-like muck, Cantrell had driven to a Super Stop 'n Shop he knew was open all night to buy a roll of electrical tape and an alarm clock. The chubby-cheeked young clerk stopped popping her gum when she saw him. She stared in what Cantrell thought was a mixture of mirth and horror at the creature from hell who stood before her.

It was dawn by the time he had reached his condo. Cantrell took off his shoes in the foyer, undressed on his way to the kitchen and dropped all his ruined clothing (including his mud-encased loafers) into the trash compactor beneath the counter.

After putting a pot of strong coffee on the burner, he had showered quickly but thoroughly. In his study, he carefully assembled his uncomplicated bomb: a simple alarm clock timer attached to a blasting cap which in turn was connected to one small stick of dynamite.

At almost 7:00 a.m. Cantrell had finally placed his completed instrument of minor destruction into the cloth shoe bag with corded drawstrings in which he had formerly stored his Gucci loafers. He had rearranged the files in his briefcase to make a snug cradle for the apparatus.

His appearance at the radio station had been greeted with knowing approval by the skeleton crew broadcasting the Sunday morning public affairs programs. Cantrell often came to the station early on game days to do last minute research on the team the Titans were playing. The crew hadn't seemed to know he had been fired. He had walked down the stairs to the basement where the archive tapes were stored and where no one else ever ventured on Sunday.

He had driven home at 9:30 feeling certain the damage from the bomb would be confined to the immediate area and that no one would be hurt. He had also felt confident that the threat of further explosions would be sufficient to keep people away from the building.

Cantrell was aware that his penchant for revenge— an often petty and irrational passion— had cost him two wives and had made him many enemies. He was a proud, stubborn man, and he knew it.

At the top level of the stadium, the elevator doors opened to reveal Cantrell's stout engineer, Harvey Bruder. "Oh boy, Howard, I thought you weren't coming! I really thought that after all these years you were finally going to miss one." The usually calm Bruder was now biting his thumb. "Robinson is already in your booth. He's got to be on the field in fifteen minutes. Where the hell have you been?"

"Haven't you heard, Harvey? I've been shit-canned. This is my last game." Cantrell searched Bruder's bland, Germanic features for a spark of compassion, a hint of understanding. He should have known better.

"Yeah, I just heard something about that. But I've got a job to do, Howard. And so do you. Those radio waves aren't going to stop emanating from our tower, you know." Harvey Bruder entered the booth adjoining Cantrell's and put on his head set which he used as ear plugs rather than as a listening device. Even though Bruder's confessed habit of operating his control panel without ever listeninq to the actual broadcast was essential to Cantrell's plan, he disliked the implications of being tuned out by his own engineer.

Through the small window in the door, Cantrell watched Bruder's chubby fingers caress the dials. Fuck him, Cantrell thought. Fuck that fat, robot bastard. Fuck them all. And as he unlocked the door to his booth, which could only be opened from the inside without a key, he heard the faint wail of sirens. His bomb had indeed exploded on time.

"Hi'ya Howie. How's it goin', ol' buddy? You're a little late, ain't you?" The petulance in Spunky Robinson's voice denied his wide grin. His squinty-eyed, weather-worn face was as mobile and deceptive as his fingers when he flashed the "steal" sign.

Cantrell nodded hello, thinking how ludicrous the beer-bellied, fifty-year-old Robinson appeared in a tight-fitting, double knit baseball uniform. He sat down, clipped on his mike and then clipped one to Robinson's shirt. The booth was a cube about the size of a walk-in closet and two men, particularly two tall men like Cantrell and Robinson, were cramped for leg room. In fact, Cantrell always felt claustrophobic when, as now, he was forced to face away from the open end, away from the field. Even though the left wall was half window, he didn't feel it expanded the booth; it only revealed the stolid Bruder at his control panel.

Cantrell noticed Bruder gesturing excitedly toward the red light which was flashing to signify they were on the air. "Good afternoon baseball fans. This is Howard Cantrell, Voice of the Toledo Titans, welcoming you to another addition of Dugout Poop. Today we've got a real turd for you, Titan field manager Skunky Robinson. We'll be asking him some pretty intimate questions right after this important message." Cantrell paused for a fraction of a second and glanced into Robinson's open mouth. A plug of well-chewed tobacco rested on his tongue.

Cantrell raised his voice an octave and continued. "Are you drowning in debt? Do those bills seem to keep coming no matter how hard you try to keep your head above water? Well, don't give up the ship. There's someone in Toledo who is willing and able to come to your rescue. Friendly Bob King has money to loan you. The kind of money that can bail you out from under the flood of car payments, furniture duns or appliance repair bills. Fifty to five hundred dollars are only as far from you as your telephone. Why not call Bob at 555-L-O-A-N and arrange for a loan by phone. Remember, Toledo legend friendly Bob King, 555-L-O-A-N, has money to loan you...and interest rates that will break your fucking back."

Cantrell again looked at Robinson and lowered his voice to its previous level. "Well Spongey, welcome to Dugout Poop."

"That's Spunky," Robinson shot back annoyed, but he quickly regained his composure. "Gee, Howie, I never knew you was such a card. Tell me, I want the truth now, we ain't really on the air, are we?" Robinson grinned knowingly, confident it was all a gag, a practical joke he had easily seen through.

"As a matter of fact, Spanky, we *are* on the air." Cantrell looked at Robinson earnestly. Robinson searched the room blankly for help. "What's that brown stuff running from your mouth?" Cantrell asked disgustedly.

Robinson instinctively reached for his chin. "Oh that, that's just a little juice from my Bull Durham plug, is all. Care for some?"

"That's a pretty disgusting habit for a man in a managerial position. It stains your teeth, makes your breath smell bad, and makes you sound like an idiot."

Robinson's neck redened, "Now, hold on, boy. There ain't nothin' wrong with a good chew. If it was good enough for ol' Ty Cobb, Pepper Martin and Nellie Fox, well then I guess it's good enough for ol' Spunky Robinson, too. It's a *real man's* habit. You don't see no women or children chewin' no tobacco, do you?" He sat back in his chair and folded his arms, satisfied.

"Speaking of women and children, Punky, the word is out around the league that you're a closet pederast."

"That's a gol-durned, bald-faced lie. Everbody knows I'm a God-fearin' Southern Baptist." Robinson paused and screwed his face up, genuinely puzzled. "But what's that got to do with women and children?"

Cantrell smiled and leaned towards him. "They say you mess around with the batboys and younger players, Punky. Is there any truth to that?"

"Wait a minute. Wait just one blessed minute. You ain't talkin' to no hayseed, boy. I know my baseball rights and I know my radio rights. I ain't got to answer no question that might intend to recriminate me." Robinson squirmed in his seat, but set his jaw.

"In Albany, they say you're especially fond of shortstop Jesus Allente. Do you want to comment on that?" Cantrell purposely pronounced the player's name "Gee-zus" to get a rise out of Robinson.

Robinson suddenly jumped up, enraged. "Now you've gone too far!" he shouted, clutching at his mike. "First off, that's Hey-Zeus not Jesus. Hey-Zeus. Them stupid Port-O-Ricans oughta know better than to name a half-assed utility infielder after our Lord and God. It's down right un-American. And second off, and here's where you really showed you ain't only not a good American, you ain't even a good Titan, neither one... You know as well as I do that Hey-Zeus is a Niggerbocker, I mean Knickerbocker. And the owners got strict rules against patronizing with the enemy. I just want the American people to know that I, Elbert Spunky Robinson, swear on a stack of living Bibles as high as a pop-up that calls for the infield fly rule, I do solemnly swear I ain't never patronized with no enemy ball players, managers, batboys and\or fans. And that's God's own truth on earth as it is in heaven." He turned to Cantrell and said menacingly, "And I'd smash your God-damned city face in if I didn't have to go downstairs and rile up my troops." Robinson tore the mike from his shirt and stormed out of the booth.

Cantrell controlled the laughter which was in his throat so he could speak distinctly, soberly. "Well, baseball fans, that was our very own Titan manager, Spunky Robinson. He left too soon for me to thank him for being on the show, but we'll see that his gift is waiting for him when he gets home tonight. That gift is something for the whole family, folks. A shoe box brim full of hard-core pornography from the Double X Book and Novelty Shop at 311 Elm right here in Toledo. I've paged through some of this stuff, and it's really first rate. There's an eight-pager in there with Dick Tracy ramming it home to Aunt Fritzi that's sure to be a collector's item. This gift has been donated by the Double X Book and Novelty Shop at 311 Elm for the advertising value received. Stay tuned to this station for today's game between the Titans and the Albany Knickerbockers right after these messages."

Cantrell switched off his mike and swung around in his swivel chair to the counter that faced the field. Ordinarily the air-time would now be filled with advertising jingles, a station break, the time and weather, all originating from the downtown studio. The knowledge that it was just dead airtime because of the bomb he had planted gave Cantrell a feeling of power and pleasure.

For the first time he was able to take a good look at the shirt-sleeved crowd through his binoculars. He estimated there were fifteen to twenty thousand fans in the half-filled stadium. Many of them had Walkman radios and most of them were twisting dials or pounding the sides with their palms. They could neither understand nor, apparently, bear the silence. Stupid bastards, Cantrell thought. They had come to watch a baseball game and yet had brought radios to hear him describe what they were seeing. Stupid bastards.

At exactly one o'clock he put on his headset and switched on his mike. "Good afternoon baseball fans, this is Howard Cantrell welcoming you to the sports voice of Toledo, Station K-R-A-S. It's a beautiful July Sunday in Toledo, perfect weather for baseball. If you couldn't make it to Hoover Memorial Stadium today, I hope you've got a big blue can of Seinsheimer beer in one hand and a woman with big tits in the other. Unless you happen to be a woman. In which case you can use your own imagination. Hey, I'm as politically correct as the next guy.

"We should have a real barn-burner today between the league-leading Albany Knickerbockers and our own cellar-dwelling Toledo Titans. We'll be back in a minute with the starting lineups for today's game; but first these few words about the beer that made Oblong, Illinois famous."

Cantrell paused and added a thick German accent to his speech. "Un 1872 un habitual drunk, Adolph Seinsheimer vas exiled from da Fattaland. He immigrated to America und settelt in Oblonk, Illinois. Beink ambizious, und schmart, not to menzion shirsty (Illinois vas a dry shtate un 1872), Herr Seinsheimer zoon eshtablisht his own brewery. He ust a shtrange, totally oonique vater, vich he zaid came from Zeleshtial Shprings deep beneat' his plant. Axzually his brewery vas located rright abof da firsht city zewer zyshtem un Illinois. Und dat brewery ist shtill dere, brewink Seinsheimer beer da ol fashiont, Oblonk, Illinois vay. Zo, da nex time your frien' zays his bik bleu can of Seinsheimer tashtes like shitz, he might be abzolutely rright." Cantrell turned his head away from the mike and coughed.

In his normal radio voice, "Well baseball fans, at this time it's customary for us to play and sing the National Anathema. But since nobody, including me, can really sing the high notes at the `rockets red glare, the bombs bursting in air' part, I'm going to ask our own terrifically talented organist, Freda Finebach, to play *Deutchsland Über Alles*, or better yet, the German Beer Drinking Song in honor of our wonderful team owner, Adoph Seinsheimer. Freda."

Although Cantrell couldn't see Freda Finebach in the booth beneath him, he could well imagine the perplexed expression on her face— a face so laden with cosmetics he thought it resembled a drag queen's attempt to imitate Ethel Merman. After a few seconds of silence, the uncharacteristic sound of ruffles and flourishes boomed over the sound system. The fans shot to their feet and placed their hands or held their hats over their hearts and sang "The Star Spangled Banner" as loudly and with as much emotion as they could muster, accompanied by Freda's fervent and furious hammering at the organ keys.

"Gee willikers, that was great folks. I'm going to have to fight through these goose bumps to give you today's starting lineups. Here goes: starting at shortstop and batting in the leadoff spot for our Titans will be hot-hitting Tony Benzaro. Tony has one hit in his last thirty-seven trips to the plate, and in my opinion that hit should have been scored an error. If you keep up that kind of hitting kid, they'll start calling you good-fielding Tony Benzaro. And pretty soon you'll be on a bus to Birmingham. Batting second, is our own Columbian Snowbird, right fielder, Juan 'Jumpin' Jack Flash' Fernandez. There has been a rumor that Juan's green card will be revoked at the end of this season. But he says that there is no truth to it. Jumpin' Jack insists he's clean and that he's crazy on the Red, White and Blue, even though he is being shadowed by narcs and his phone is reportedly tapped.

"Toledo's own Johnny Power is batting third and will patrol left field as is the usual happenstance." Suddenly there was a banging at his door and Cantrell turned to see a huge, menacing, pink face staring at him through the square window. Then he heard the loud thud of a vicious kick. Cantrell quickly spun back around. For the first time he noticed that the fans in the stadium were gathered in groups around anyone holding a radio. And they were all staring up toward his booth.

"I don't have much time left, folks. They're coming to get me. But I want you to know that I have it on good authority, from the horse's mouth, as it were, yes, from Johnny Power's own wife...I want you to know, baseball fans, that Johnny Power is a bad lay. Do you hear me? Johnny Power is a bum fuck! And what's more— are you listening out there in radio land?— baseball is a little boys' game! Have you got that? Baseball is only..." At that instant the door to the booth was kicked open and a broad-shouldered policeman, gun in hand, stormed in followed by one of the owner's sons, Rudolph Seinsheimer. The cop stood before him for a moment, trembling with what Cantrell knew was either fear or rage, his gun pointed squarely at Cantrell's groin. Of a sudden it occurred to Cantrell that an explanation was in order. He reached for the telegram that was in his inside jacket pocket.

"The commie sumbitch's got a gun," Rudolph Seinsheimer screamed. Cantrell quickly withdrew his hand and shot both arms in the air, but it was too late. The young patrolman rushed him and caught Cantrell flush in the chest with a powerful shoulder block. The force of the blow lifted Cantrell off his feet and propelled him out of the booth.

He tumbled onto the tough nylon screen designed to protect the fans behind home plate from foul balls. Slowly at first, and then with increasing velocity, the arms and legs, the undignified heap, rolled down the screen. The hitherto silent, stupefied spectators suddenly, and in unison (as though on cue), began the sound they always made when a foul ball rolled down the screen: "WooooOOPS."

Cantrell's fall came to an abrupt halt when he reached the dip in the screen where it was attached to the backstop. He mentally surveyed the damage as he peered over the edge: a drop of ten feet to the artificial turf. Other than being slightly out of breath from the blow to his chest and a little dizzy from the roll down the screen, Cantrell decided he was unhurt. He was, however, chagrined to find that the K-R-A-S sports logo, which he had helped design, was torn loose from his blazer. The patch featured a crown from his British ancestors' heraldic crest, the station's call letters, and crossed baseball bats cradling a baseball in a glove all stitched in gold on a field of maroon.

Cantrell lay perfectly still. For ten full seconds the crowd was silent. No one even coughed. The silence was broken by a single shout of joy from the left field bleachers. That shout was echoed by someone in the right field pavilion. A general whooping and stomping soon followed, resembling the religious rapture of a captivated audience in an evangelist's tent. As Cantrell glanced around, he saw women and young girls crying, hugging whoever happened to be sitting next to them. Men in sport coats good naturedly pummeled the backs of guys wearing nylon shirts with bowling team names emblazoned across the front. An electric good will, an unspeakable joy seemed to fill the hearts of the crowd.

During the bedlam, Cantrell pulled himself up so he could see the whole stadium. The battery powered golf cart, which was used to deliver relief pitchers from the center field bullpen to the mound, was driven onto the turf. The cart stopped at home plate.

Suddenly, from the Titan dugout, sprang a husky young man dressed in blue. At first Cantrell, who was a little nearsighted, thought the guy was an umpire, but the shiny brass on his chest and his distinctive cap revealed his identity to Cantrell and the crowd. Flanked by two blonde, teenaged "ball girls" clad in Titan blue and white cheerleader skirts, the cop who had assaulted Cantrell sprinted to the electric cart. The crowd quieted to a low murmur as someone wearing an American Legion hat handed the patrolman the Stars and Stripes.

From his precarious perch on the screen, the forgotten and bemused Cantrell surveyed the scene as though he were watching a pageant he had helped plan. Over the sound system came a spirited rendition of "America the Beautiful" played by the redoubtable Freda Finebach.

Hearing the music, the eager young policeman began to wave the flag vigorously as he was slowly driven around the perimeter of the artificially surfaced field.

And the crowd went wild.

ABOUT THE AUTHOR

Spiro Athanas was born in 1942 in St. Louis, Missouri. He attended Washington University in St. Louis on a Frances scholarship. He has taken creative writing courses at Washington University, the University of Cincinnati and Indiana University. His work has been published in the Ball State University *Forum* and in an anthology entitled *Ethnic American Short Stories* edited by Katherine D. Newman. A lifelong resident of the midwest, Mr. Athanas has been an advertising copywriter and a carpenter in St. Louis, the director of a contemporary art gallery in Indianapolis, an office equipment salesman and sales manager in Cincinnati and Louisville, a marketing executive for food service companies in Louisville and Indiana, and the owner of a number of franchised restaurants in central Indiana. He sold his businesses in 1994 and now lives, writes and pursues his other avocations in Bloomington, Indiana. His wife, Jo Ann, is a CPA and the controller of a local healthcare company. His son, Josef, is a lawyer in Chicago.